BOOKS BY HANS KONING
(a.k.a. Hans Koningsberger)

Fiction:
The Kleber Flight   1981
The Petersburg-Cannes Express   1975
Death of a Schoolboy   1974
The Revolutionary   1967
I Know What I'm Doing   1964
A Walk with Love and Death   1961
An American Romance   1960
The Affair   1958

Nonfiction:
A New Yorker in Egypt   1976
Columbus, His Enterprise   1976
The Almost World   1971
The Future of Che Guevara   1971
Along the Roads of Russia   1968
Love and Hate in China   1966

Translations:
From the Dutch:
Maria Dermout's "The Ten Thousand Things" and
    "Yesterday"   1958, 1960
From the French:
Carlo Coccioli's "Manuel the Mexican"   1961

The Kleber Flight

The
Kleber
Flight

Hans Koning

ATHENEUM   NEW YORK   1981

LIBRARY OF CONGRESS CATALOGING IN PUBLICATION DATA

Koning, Hans, ———
   The Kleber flight.

  I. Title.
PS3561.046K5   1981   813'.54   81-66025
ISBN 0-689-11221-1   AACR2

Published simultaneously in Canada by McClelland and Stewart Ltd.
Composed by American–Stratford Graphic Services, Brattleboro, Vermont
Manufactured by R. R. Donnelley & Sons Co., Harrisonburg, Virginia
Designed by Mary Cregan
First Edition

For M.S.

"The highest themes: love, arms and virtue."

DANTE, *De Vulgari Eloquentia*

The Kleber Flight

1.

IN THE WEEK OF April 7, 1969, I made love to five different women. Last night, rattling around in my room and at a loss what to do, I ended up looking through my old diaries, *Week-at-a-Glance*'s from 1960 on, and came upon this perhaps not so fascinating item. I had written it down in my private code which consists simply of the Greek alphabet for the English words. It cheered me up when I came to the entry, written in under the Saturday of that week, *ius φεεκ ι cκρευεδ φιφε φομεν*. The *u* in screwed substitutes for the *w*, a letter the Greeks did not have.

I have not used that little code for years but when I did use it, it was for myself only, to tone down such statements in my own eyes. I once had a very jealous girlfriend but she was jealous in a proprietary manner and not because she was much interested in me. She would surely never have bothered to look in my diaries. The same is true for a wife I had for three years (not as long as the jealous girlfriend actually). The Greek letters were to give myself the feeling that I was not showing off, was not thinking, "Look what a dashing fellow I am." And the five-women entry cheered me up only as it seemed to show that people must have been pleased with me and I must have had a lot of happy energy to cope with the running around and the subterfuge needed, that week in April now more than a decade ago. It surprised me, especially for the year 1969, which I remember all in all as a terrible time.

When I had gone through the lot, up to the 1980 diary I am using now, I went back to the 1969 one and tore out that page. I stared at it, and although I tried hard, I could not remember a single name or face of any of those five. I knew how I had lived that year, a second-floor one-room apartment on the south side of East 61st Street, with a kind of bamboo folding door screening off the kitchen and my desk chair looking down upon the awning across the street of a doctors' building, with ambulance parking where the doorman often let me put my car. In the end I came upon one image in my memory, of my bending over a girl lying on my bed, and her looking up at my body and then at my face. It had been midday, lunch hour.

It is a matter of age, I belong to a generation born before World War II or better, before Pearl Harbor and we felt, or somehow I felt, that "making it" was a big event, no matter how it may have seemed afterward, indifferent, terrible, nice; each new—new what? not conquest, I'm not so old that I would think in such terminology—each new intimacy with someone who had been a stranger just before, was amazing, was to be chalked up against the passage of time. A monument more-durable-than-bronze.

Presumably I have gone on feeling like that, even when people put making love more and more in one class with jogging. Presumably that is why all the entries in those twenty years of diaries seemed to relate to lovemaking; I mean the special entries, not my appointments and such. Things written down to be remembered some future time.

That future time was last night, then. Here was the essence of perhaps half my adult life. But was that all the emotional luggage I had meant to carry through the years? I had lived from day to day, each day for itself, like a cat or a dog or a child, with nothing to show for it but those contacts with bodies which must have been stroked and invaded so many times since, in whose minds and on whose skins I had not left a single trace. Sitting at my window, the light in the sky fading, too lazy to get up and turn on the lamp, I was surprised I had not seen before how depressing this record was, not much better than if I had listed the meals I had eaten. A record of bodily functions, a life on the sidelines. I took the diaries and that idiotic torn-out page and went downstairs to throw the lot in the garbage can which I had already put out. Half an hour later I went down and fished them out, tore up the front pages which had my name, and dropped them back in.

The following morning, the morning after the diaries evening that is, I woke up sorry I had done that. When I was outside ready to go to work, I lifted the lid off the garbage can to salvage those twenty years after all. But the can had already been emptied.

I drove off under a sky which was almost painfully blue, a tight blue, but when I had reached Merrick Road it turned black in one minute and by the time I had parked, it was pouring. A dark autumn morning, with the rain coming down so hard now that my office windows were opaque with water. The office, a prefab building holding my room, a waiting room with a Coke machine and a tableful of magazines, a closet, and a washroom, was the home of the Seataugh, Long Island, Flying School. It sat at the edge of the airfield with a parking lot on one side and beyond that, wasteland up to the Sound. I was the office manager. Manager in a manner of speaking: there was no one else around to manage.

At that time the owner of the school had stopped appearing and telephoned in once a day only. He was the kind of man who had a dozen enterprises going simultaneously and the school had not answered the expectations he had when

[5]

he bought it. Our maintenance and the instructors, all that part of it, were across the field, and the canteen, too, was more than a mile's walk away. Thus whole days went by without my seeing a soul.

The weather forecast had been for late summer sunshine, and for once we had been completely booked with lessons. I spent some hours on the telephone arranging cancellations and I got hold of every student up until two o'clock. My little radio announced twenty-four hours of rain and wind and I thought it would be nice to cancel the whole day and get out. But as I had my hand on the receiver, the telephone rang. It was my boss, calling to assure me it was going to clear and I was not to accept any cancellations of bookings for after three.

"But I haven't heard from Joseph or from Benson," I answered. Those were our two instructors. When they were both busy, we could get still another man on loan from Zahns Airport. All the school owned at this point were three Piper Tomahawks and a Piper Arrow Four.

"I'll make sure one of them will show up," the boss said. "Don't you go home, David."

So I dialed our own number instead, left the receiver off the hook, and walked out onto the field toward the bay.

A high wind had begun blowing, tugging at my coat and blinding me with rain. No one was about, there was no sound but of the rain and the wind, and just barely the far rumble of the JFK traffic which even a day like this did not ground. Clouds were racing across a higher layer of gray, seagulls stood still against the storm and screamed. I went to where the oil-stained pavement ended at the swamp which makes up the shore there. Oyster Bay had waves like the sea that morning, glaring in the false light filtering through the clouds, and the sky looked as it does in old prints of shipwrecks.

On the ground around me it was present time, empty oil

drums, debris from plastic bottles to old tires and a cap-sized, trackless bulldozer, with the tall swamp weeds waving around them. Paper, bits of newspaper and brown wrapping paper, were blowing through all this, got stuck, flapped wildly, and blew on again. I turned my face into the wind and it all became hidden in a curtain of rain washing my face, and I was standing in a dome of gray air and water, and saw just what the first man who ever stood on that beach must have seen, or equally well what the last man will see.

There will be a last man or woman or child in all human history to stand there and look at Oyster Bay. It may have a different name then but never mind that, there is nothing vague about the moment, one specific person will have the last look at this scene in all the history of the universe. The idea unnerved me. I could not stay with ideas like that, I had to get on to something else. Bodies usually, bodies are our best defense.

2.

I HAVE READ EVERYTHING and I have seen nothing.

Except women. That is why I think about them so much, too much. To see a young woman naked, with the knowledge that you are going to make love to her, seems the happiest experience on earth, antidote to everything, even to death.

It is not that crazy. In travel books, nineteeth-century ones, not modern ones, which I do not like, the romance and the adventure is not the Pyramids or the Kurdistan bandits but women—even those hardly seen. And think of

Sterne, *Sentimental Journey*, all that travel to almost touch the chambermaid's belly. In a Russian novel, I believe Dostoyevski, I read of a man thinking, "Anatomy is our only salvation." He meant a woman's body, or so I understood it. I was in high school when I read that and those words excited me more than any of the nudie magazines we passed around. I could not read on, I had to make myself come.

That idea seemed a revelation, and I wondered if it worked the other way around, for a woman thinking of men. It was hard to imagine it would. I do not think any of us had read a word of Freud's but in our afterschool discussions we held forth about longing back for the womb. It explained why men wanted it so much more than women, which is what we all assumed. A woman's body was not just the mirror of a man's, we were all sure of its near-surrealist attraction.

I have since vainly tried to find the Dostoyevski passage, I remembered it came before the hero had an obscene dream in which a child of five or six tried to seduce him. The written language of his century was so chaste, it makes the desire in it more of a shock. Longing must have been more intense in that world where you did not even get to see a woman's ankles, where nice girls kept on their shifts when they took a bath by themselves. Think of it, think of marrying a sixteen-year-old virgin as middle-aged widowers did in those days when they had used up one wife in childbirth, sitting through the ceremony in high collar and gloves and tight shoes, and then suddenly being alone with her and have her take off all those skirts and flounces and stand there, those curves coming together at her center, a nude, untouched young girl. Legal rape by a man who would have a red, congested face and a potbelly and who would be burping and pissing in a chamber pot afterward.

[8]

Once on Third Avenue I was accosted by a girl who just said, "Wanna come?" and I followed her into a kind of massage parlor above a delicatessen. She stared out of the window while she handled me. She looked fourteen. For about an hour afterward I felt guilty and thought it was unforgivable that I had profited from a kind of slavery right in the middle of New York. Then I went back to feeling that those little hands with their bitten nails on me had been breathtaking.

I do not know what the truth of it is, how the same thing can be empty and cheap and then again as important as dying.

3.

I HAD STAYED OUT too long on the Oyster Bay shore and when I got back in the office I was soaked through and shivering like a rat. I tried to dry myself off with the little washroom towel and I put my shoes on a newspaper in front of the electric fire. I ate my sandwich and a candy bar and read my book. The Coke machine owed me about five dollars and I tried to get a can out by kicking and tilting, but without success.

At three it was still raining, and at half past three too, though the wind had dropped. Neither of the two instructors had telephoned in and the student for three o'clock had not appeared. I was about to close up when I heard a car, and then a woman entered the waiting room. I waved at her to come into the office, but she stood still near the door and hesitated. She stared at me or that is how it looked from what I could see of her face between wet strands of hair and the scarf she had around her head. I got up from behind my desk and she looked at my feet.

I said, "Excuse the socks. My shoes had to dry."

She still did not move. She was frowning now.

It was not unusual for people to hesitate this way. We got students who did not come for the love of flying but because they had been told that lessons would help against being afraid of airliners. Sometimes it works.

I tried a smile. "Come in and dry your coat," I said. "It's warmer in here. Not much, but noticeably."

She did not move but seemed to reach a decision. "I'm booked for four o'clock," she told me. "My first lesson."

I put my shoes back on and got out a new Pilot's Log and Rating Record for her. She was on my reservation sheet as Mrs. Beatrix Orme, with no address or telephone number.

"I'm David Lum," I said. "You should have phoned, Mrs. Orme. The weather is terrible."

"I tried. Your line is always busy."

"I'm sorry. But it's not really a day to start. The instructors haven't even come in."

She seemed extraordinarily disappointed. "Are you sure?" she asked. "I saw a lot of people back there where the road passes the hangars. It's a long drive for me to get here."

"That's not us, those men you saw, that's the Republic factory. They build planes."

"I want to learn very fast," she said. "I need a license within a couple of weeks."

"A couple of weeks?"

"Yes. For a job."

"A couple of weeks . . . what kind do you need? There's the private pilot's license, and a commercial license, and then—but you're not thinking ahead to flying for an airline?"

"I guess just the private one," she answered. "Where you

can fly by yourself, and where they'll rent you a plane. Please call and see if I can start, I'd be very grateful."

I decided to telephone the canteen across the field on the off-chance, since Mrs. Orme was so disappointed, or more than that, crestfallen. And they told me they had seen Joseph and fetched him for me. Yes, he said, he'd be glad to take someone up. "Your rotten boss always drags me down here," he said, "just wasting my time. Let's make some dough. Even if the lady gets airsick."

So I filled in a Log and Rating and showed her how to drive back to the main hangar. She booked another lesson for the next day, at nine in the morning. "And each day from there on," she said. "I'll pay for ten lessons now."

"It's better if you come back here after your flight," I answered. "People usually want to see first how they like it."

"I'll like it fine. I'll pay with cash."

4.

I WAS SITTING in the movie house of Rockville Centre and waiting for the lights to go out, or rather, to dim. They were afraid there that if they made the place really dark the customers would take it apart. I always sit way up front and no one sat near me. The theater was three-quarters empty anyway. A smell of faded plush and old popcorn, a screen which was torn at the bottom, and the sound system playing an organ rendition of "Whispering." "Whispering"? That's what we played in the high school band. No, grade school.

This whole movie-house scene is like a Saturday afternoon in Bridgeport, Connecticut, in the fifties, except that when I was in junior high, we paid forty cents instead of three dollars.

The past keeps reemerging. It started with those diaries. That same 1969 *Week-at-a-Glance* had had an entry in October, saying "Job." It had been scratched out later, and a star filled in with red marker drawn on the day. I had gone past it without much thought; I knew it was connected with Chicago and with two young girls, one girl really, whose name had been Jean. I did not know why it came back to me in the half light of the movie house.

An autumn day in Chicago, of violent rainstorms just like this day at the flying school. I had been on my way to a job interview. One moment I was walking down an empty street and next thing there was a line of police and one of them hit me in the face. That is to say, I always assumed he was a cop although he was in civilian clothes. He gave me a nosebleed, which was particularly maddening as I was wearing a suit and a button-down shirt and tie, because of the job of course. Not only had that attire failed to keep the police away from me, but the blood got all over my raincoat and on the shirt and the jacket, too. If I remembered rightly, it was a nice, light gray jacket. I also saw myself in a restaurant washroom trying to get out the stains, and a waiter coming in and telling me, "The boss says, 'Beat it.'"

That was the first time I felt on the wrong side of the fence with not the bad guys but the good guys my enemies. I must have led a pretty sheltered life; I was twenty-eight in the fall of '69.

This is not to make a drama out of it; I knew it was nothing. I had watched the news on television for the past decade. The police had not even wanted to run me in. It was a mistake and they ignored me once I was standing there dabbing my nose with my handkerchief and the man who had hit me had vanished. It was more complex: a coming together of feelings and of things happening. I had been out of a job for some time, I was in a city I did not know, having my job appointment messed up—no, not even that. I could have gone, bloodstains and all, and explained; the job man might even have been sympathetic, might have taken me home and asked his wife to get me one of his shirts, might have had me stay for dinner.

Maybe it was connected with the mood in the streets of the city that day, the kids with their windbreakers with little flags sewn on and the cops with their visered helmets like comics spacemen, the cold wind and rain from the lake (I never saw the lake, but everyone there talking about the weather always said it came from the lake). I had been oblivious to it, absorbed by myself, but once I had been stopped dead by that punch on the nose it got to me, as in a car on a hot day the heat hits you at a traffic stop. Except that this was not heat but cold. A bad feeling. Feeling old. Or as if America had suddenly become an old country. That is what I thought later, when I had forgotten the circumstances but remembered my mood.

The meeting with the two girls later plays its part in it, too.

Anyway, I did not go to the job appointment. I did not even phone.

Next, I remembered, I had been walking down Haymarket Square. I recalled the name because I had tried to get into a drugstore there for a cup of coffee and they were about to lock up. When they saw me with my blood stains they locked the door in my face and turned the sign from "Open" to "Closed."

I had stood there a while scowling at the man behind the door and tempted to do some banging on the glass. That place was called Haymarket Drugs. But I walked on, and then I passed the two girls. When I glanced at them I saw that tears were running down their faces.

They looked back at me, at the same time defiantly and pathetically. "Do you need help?" I asked.

It had been dark by then in Chicago. The street lights were reflected in the pavement, there were rainbow shimmers everywhere as from oil. The rain, which had come down all day, had ended at dusk.

I had looked at a street lamp swaying on a cable high above the square; I had half-closed my eyes and thought how these girls, crying, would see the light all with halos and clusters of rays.

All this came back to me in the Rockville movie house eleven years later to the accompaniment of "Whispering." One of the two girls, I now realized, had been the Mrs. Beatrix Orme who had just begun her flying lessons.

5.

AFTER I HAD ASKED those girls, "Do you need help?" they had taken in my appearance, and had said, "Yes. Please."

We had turned down a side street where there were no police cars and gone into a coffee shop. They calmed down, and told me they had slept in a church basement for two nights, but that morning the police had raided the place, turned them out, and thrown their packs and possessions out after them into the muddy yard. One of the two had a wicked gash over her eye. They had return tickets for the bus to Chagrin Falls, Ohio, where they went to school, but they had no money and the only through connection left at 9:30 in the morning. Their friends were in jail.

We had hamburgers and then we walked to my hotel.

They went up together with my key, and I hung around a while in the lobby and bought the paper and then went up too. No one bothered about us.

We took turns taking baths and they helped me clean my clothes a bit. We were too bushed to go anywhere or even to sit around; we pulled the twin beds apart and they crept in one and I in the other. We left the light on in the bathroom, and from under the covers they took off their underwear and tossed it into the chair. One of them stuck her foot out from under the blanket and showed me it was black and blue where they had kicked her.

Once in bed, we had talked a long time in the half-lit room. One girl started crying again, but her friend and I soothed her. They were both shaken, not because of their being penniless in a big city, not because they had been hurt, and not even because most of their stuff had been lost. Worse had happened to them on hikes and camping trips, they assured me.

Why then?

"I never knew that people are like that," one said. "I mean, I do know. I watch the news. But then again I didn't know."

"I even read the news," the other said.

"I did not know for real," her friend said. "I didn't know with my innards. Do you understand?" They both laughed about that "innards."

Yes I did understand, though I had not found out any earlier than they. Days like that October Chicago day must have shown whole battalions of people, suddenly, how it would feel not to be welcome in this world.

We did not talk about the war. When I half-apologetically started to say something about my not being involved in antiwar demonstrations, they stopped me dead by announcing, "Old people never bother," and "My parents are the same."

We talked about the human race though. Was there any future for us? Why were we such a mixed-up bunch? I asked them what they studied. "Studied? We're in high school." I was almost twice as old as they were.

It did not matter, no one was holding forth, they were wise, those girls, or maybe the better word is, unphoney. Once or twice I started telling them something for effect but checked myself in time—they had that kind of influence. The girl with the black and blue ankle fell asleep first, and the other one and I talked on very softly. She was the one called Jean. It was Jean who said something about many of their neighbors in Ohio being the second or third generation of folk who had run away from the old empires of Europe with their ever-present armies, and how sad it would be if America now became like that.

Then she said, "If you want to go turn off the bathroom light, I'll close my eyes," (because I had nothing on) and in the dark she said, "You can kiss me good night," and I did. Lying there in the pitch-black room, my heart was racing at the idea of those two nude girls three feet away from me, and it was not too easy to get to sleep.

The following morning I treated them to waffles and walked them to the bus depot. They told me their names, but I had only remembered "Jean." Jean was now Mrs. Beatrix Orme. Jean must have been a nickname or perhaps she had hated that "Beatrix" as a teenager.

They had sent me a postcard when they graduated from Chagrin Falls High.

She would have been surprised, Jeanie, if she had known how often I had thought about them in the first months after Chicago. That seriousness living within the glowing, unused body of a fifteen- or sixteen-year-old, with that look of scrubbed health young girls so often have in this country (especially if they are from such places as Chagrin Falls, Ohio), whose long legs I had seen only in my imagination

—it had made me feel I should aspire to playing a less negligible role in the world. But I am a passive person, and with the passage of time I forgot about it.

6.

I DID NOT SEE Beatrix Orme for several days. Once the flying students had registered and paid, there was no need for them to come to the office. But later that week, a slow, boring Thursday afternoon, I saw on the list that she had moved to the last hour in the schedule and I decided to walk over and say hello, and tell her who I was. It would be funny to dig up our Chicago evening.

I was sitting at the canteen window with the coffee which always got progressively worse through the day, when I recalled how she had stared at me when she came in to register and how she had hesitated. And I realized she already had recognized me, and had not been pleased about it. She must have been embarrassed and that was stupid. It had been such a nice memory, for me that is.

I went outside. I knew her plane was due back in and felt I would rather not meet her. I had left my car at my office because it was such bright and summery weather, and I started walking back. Benson, the younger of the two instructors, drove past me on his way to the gate and shouted, "Want a lift?" I shook my head but he stopped. I got over to his window and said, Thanks, but I liked the walk.

Our Piper Tomahawk came in just then and we both looked. "A fine landing," he said. "She's a natural, that one."

"Mrs. Orme? Is she on landings already?"

"Yes. Fastest student we ever had."

I did not wait to see her climb out but marched on. I locked up at the office and drove home.

Home, specifically, at that time was a one-room apartment over a garage, presumably built for a chauffeur, although no 1980 chauffeur would be willing to live in it. The garage was not in use but the whole place stank of gas all the same. It sat at the edge of Rockville Centre, which is more or less halfway between Brooklyn and Jones Beach.

I had become its tenant by turning over my lease of an apartment in Parkway Village to the garage owner. Parkway Village is a rather jazzy development in Queens with a long waiting list, but I had always hated living there, even when I was married. When the apartment was the only thing left of the marriage, it became even more hateful and the exchange deal seemed a bit of luck. The garage apartment was close to the flying school where I was already working, and I thought it would tide me over temporarily and nicely.

I had been married to a woman I hardly knew while I was married to her. Three years, and she had become real only on our last evening, when she told me she thought she was in love with someone in her office and wanted to be on her own to work it out.

"You're very dear to me, David," she had said, "but I have to handle this my own way."

"Have you been to bed with this man?" I had asked.

"Oh please."

"Oh please," I repeated. "Have you or haven't you?"

"What does it matter? Perhaps once."

"Or twice? Was it nice? Did you come?"

"Please," she said again. And then, "Do *you* want me? Now? Come on, don't sulk."

I did want her, more than I had in a long time. How predictable and stupid we are. I walked out and slept in my office at Seataugh and the next morning, although I had rushed back at dawn, she had already packed up and gone. A week later I was out, too, and lived over the garage. That was a year ago. Nothing is as permanent as the temporary, and I did not notice the gas smell any more.

7.

BEATRIX ORME TELEPHONED ME late in the evening, at the garage apartment. Joseph, her instructor, had given her the number, she said. She took me very much by surprise. "I guess you want to change tomorrow's booking," I asked, not very friendly. No, that wasn't it. She had seen me walk away as she landed.

"Eh, yes—I had some business with Mr. Benson. He is the other instructor."

"Yes, I know."

"I hear you are doing very well."

"Yes, I guess so."

A pause. I thought I should help her out.

"Mrs. Orme," I said, "I know we know each other. It's long ago. I'm sorry if the idea embarrasses you. Please forget it."

"Oh no," she answered, "That's not it. That was a good time. We had a good evening in Chicago. I've often thought about it."

"I thought you—"

"No, I don't," she cut in.

Another silence.

"I phoned you," she finally said, "because in Chicago I called myself Jean."

"Well, it's surely no business of the Seataugh Flying School what you want to call yourself."

"Yes, true. I just figured—" She hesitated again. "Had you remembered my name?" she asked.

"I guess so."

"Oh."

"I'm glad the school agrees with you," I went on. "That's to say, I was told you're the fastest student we've ever had. And that landing today—after just three half-hours—"

She laughed now. "Can you fly?"

I said, "Not really. I never got near a license."

She waited again, I did not know for what.

"What else, Jean?" I asked. "Do you need help?" I remembered those Chicago words, and so did she. She laughed again. "No," she said. "Not now. Good night, Mr. Lum."

Jean. Jean who? Now her last name came back to me. Jean More.

More—Orme. She had married a man whose name was an anagram of her own. Funny coincidence.

I went to my kitchen counter and opened a can of franks and beans. Then I thought, It's not a coincidence; people who change their names rarely do it drastically, they like to hold on a bit to the old ones. Some stick to the same initials. Jean More had done a reshuffle, I was of a sudden sure of it. She was neither Beatrix nor Orme, and she had been upset about my knowing her.

I worried about it, for her sake. I decided to go over to her side of the field one day soon and ask. She wasn't fifteen any more but she had sounded very uncertain on that telephone.

Half an hour later I knew what it was all about. A picture of her emerged in my mind, a picture I had seen years ago in the *Times*. The memory of it had been buried, perhaps through my not thinking of her name: I think in words more than in images. The story with the picture had said that Jean More was wanted by the FBI, possibly even that she was on the Ten Most Wanted list.

Once I knew the reason for her behavior, I felt relieved and, odd as it may seem, I was not worried about it. It had been some kind of political business. In those days (and for all I know, still) the FBI got more worked up about radical students than about billion-dollar crime syndicates. Jean should have known that I would not care and that the idea of denouncing her would not enter my mind.

I did a lot of thinking about her that evening. The faces of those two girls which had become superimposed in my mind and blended into one, separated themselves. Jean was the girl with the gash over her eye, the one who had calmed down first, the one who had said, "You can kiss me good night." Eleven years ago. And here she was back.

8.

THE NEXT MORNING I decided to tell her, the first chance I had, that I knew about that FBI business, to make sure she would not worry about my finding out her secret. But she did not telephone or come in, neither that day nor during the weekend. Monday was my day off with a part-time woman sitting in and when I came back to work after that, she still had not called.

Obviously she did not trust me and she had dropped out. I wondered why she needed a license in such a hurry, and would have liked to find her and tell her I was on her side whatever she was up to, but I did not know how to. There was no telephone listing in her old or her new name. She had paid in cash.

And then she telephoned me at the end of an afternoon, as I was standing in the doorway waiting for the call from the boss. Assuming it was he, I did not hurry to get to my desk. The sun was going in behind dark clouds at the edge of the field, making silvery edges before vanishing. It was real autumn now, feelings of cold and of darkness.

"Hello, David," she said.

I told her I was glad she called, we did not want to lose our best student.

"Well," she said, "I'm not very far away, a couple of miles down Sunrise Highway."

"What are you doing there?" I asked. She did not answer. "I'm about to close up," I said. "Why don't you come by and we will do your new bookings, and perhaps you'll have a drink with me. For old times' sake."

"All right."

She looked terrible when she showed up, pale and thin. I had my first chance to see her properly and was surprised I had not recognized her before, even with the scarf and the wet hair. For she did not seem much older than on that Chicago evening, perhaps because her face was pinched as of a very tired child.

"You haven't changed much, you know," was the first thing I said. "You still look about fifteen."

She had a little smile. "I don't really want to go anywhere," she said. "How about having some Cokes in here?"

"That machine rarely works," I answered. But she was not listening; she was staring out through the open door at the sunset and with such a miserable expression on her face that my heart sank. Don't look like that, I thought, I'll help, maybe it's my best role in life, once every ten years.

"Where did you phone from?" I asked. "Please sit down. Were you afraid of coming straight here?"

"I was at Zahns Airport, I was about to register there."

Now she smiled. "This time I was Kathleen Jacobs. But then—then I felt too goddamn tired and disheartened to go on with that, and the idea of dodging you seemed so stupid, I thought I'd come back here." She put coins in the machine and it worked. She sat down with her Coke without looking at me.

I was afraid of giving the wrong answer. I bent over and sort of patted her on the head.

"You knew, didn't you?" she asked.

"Not when you phoned that night, later. I don't care! Think of our Chicago night, and think of all the things we said! About the people running our lives, and—"

"But Jesus Christ," she said slowly. "A lot has happened since. Very much has happened. You looked so wild when you walked past us that evening, with the blood on your coat, you were flaring, like a pursued criminal."

"Flaring?"

"Yes, flaring. With your eyes, like deer do, or cats." She began to laugh now and I had to laugh with her. She sounded almost tender suddenly. "That's why I trusted you," she said.

I put four dimes in the machine but nothing happened although I kicked it so hard that it left a dent and hurt my knee. She held out her can for me, and I sat down beside her.

"Tomorrow at nine?" I asked. "I think that's your favorite hour."

"Yes. It's so still then over the bay, you have no idea. Sometimes you can follow the wake from a little boat for miles."

"And you will come and have dinner with me now?"

"I don't like going out," she said.

"Well, do you want to have dinner with me at my place? If you're free."

"If you let me buy some of it. I'm very flush these days."

"Okay. You still owe me for a hamburger and for waffles."

"Right."

9.

SHE FOLLOWED ME in her car to Rockville Centre. I took her up to my room and after she had insisted on stuffing a five-dollar bill in my pocket, I went out again to get some more food. When I came back she had tied a towel around her waist and was taking the dirty dishes out of the sink, but I stopped her. Ever since as a child I watched my divorced father come visit us and (after a few protests) have my mother feed him and sew on his buttons, I have hated that a-woman's-role stuff.

There had been very few girls in my garage apartment and those few who had been there fell into two categories, number one (totalling three) who looked around and especially smelled around and then got out fast, and number two (also about three) who did not give a damn about gasoline smells nor about anything else as long as it turned out their escort really liked making love to women and did not prefer "cutting them up with a razor or buggering them" to quote one of my visitor's precise words. Those did not need Chianti or candles, they were ready to get on with it. Nothing about that fitted in with any monument moredurable-than-bronze ideas, but then they had searched for so long that everyone and no one was a stranger to them. As for me, after that marriage of mine I had not been looking for soul mates, I had not been looking for anything. It was only that after a while sex becomes an obsession, and you have to act.

Jean's presence had no connection with all this. It was a new thing. I heated the food I had bought, no cheap TV dinners but frozen crab newburg from Stouffers, and set the table.

As if by agreement we talked about the events of the day, what was happening in the world, and did not ask about each other's lives or try to fill in all those years. That one Chicago night was too fragile to tag all that time onto.

I did ask her for the name of the other girl, which had been on the tip of my tongue for days now.

"Monica."

"Really? I was all off then."

"Yes, that's her. She went to Seattle, or a place near there. Evergreen College. We lost sight of each other."

"Chagrin Falls," I said. "I think I fell in love with that name."

"Chagrin Falls High," Jean murmured, more like a sigh.

"And you," I asked, "What is this flying job you're after?"

She shook her head. "I don't feel like talking about it, not now anyway. I feel peaceful for once."

And indeed, a particular kind of peace had come over her, visibly so. She looked different, no longer a pinched and worried child but a young woman.

"You've grown up beautifully, Jean," I said.

She closed her eyes for a moment in answer. She said, "I'm happy because not one single soul in the world knows where I am right now."

That startled me, I had forgotten the FBI. "Are they still after you?" I asked. "Shouldn't you— Do you have a lawyer? Can I do something? I didn't ask before, but only because I didn't want to pry."

She shook her head. "I didn't mean to sound like a fugitive, it is nothing dramatic. I've been on their list for years, they just forgot to take me off. Or maybe they don't have another woman, to show they're not sexists. It's just the idea. If your phone rings, or your doorbell, it can't possibly be for me. I could happily sit here for a year."

I thought about that and when she said nothing more, I answered, "Do. You're welcome."

A shadow went across her face and for a moment she had that sad child expression again. "A year is a long time," she said. And then, "Are you that lonely?"

I felt myself redden. "That's not why I offered. I offered because after that night, eleven years ago, I—" I did not know how to end that sentence. "No, I'm not lonely," I said. "I'm alone these days but it's by choice. Most of my friends came and went with the life I led, my marriage and everything. It all collapsed together. I'll get back to it, with real friends if any. Right now I'm into interior asceticism, I guess."

"Into what?"

"That's a term from some German writer. Where you're in the world but also in a monastery within yourself, sort of."

"Christ. That would be from a German writer. Is that what you want?"

"No. I'm joking. Well, not altogether. I want it in a way. I'm content on the sidelines. But I surely didn't mean a monastery like monks have."

She laughed. "A monastery with sisters of mercy."

She looked at me with such friendly eyes, she really seemed to expect an answer to that. "Oh you know," I said, "It's not easy to—in the old days you could just go to a—" I felt embarrassed. "Anyway, you can always help yourself. That's very popular these days."

"I don't know what you're talking about," she said.

"Well—*Playboy, Penthouse, She, You, Woman, Rock,*

Screw, all the magazines in our waiting room describe how to do it yourself, like, rock star so-an-so is only dating himself these days, he says it avoids hassles."

She did not smile.

"If you want to, if you really need to, you can use me," she said.

"Use you?" I repeated.

She sounded very matter-of-fact. "I'm not into lovemaking these days," she told me. "Don't ask me why not. Not now. But since we're here to help each other—I'll lend you my body if that's what you need. If you're gentle."

I leaned over to kiss her, but she moved her head. "Just my belly," she said. "Just for a little while. And you must turn off the lights and keep them off, promise."

In the dark, standing in the kitchen corner, I got out of my clothes. I made my way to the bed and found her lying on it. I hesitantly touched her, discovering that she had taken off her shoes and her jeans. The lower half of her body was naked. She said in a low, hoarse voice, "Just come in me."

She did not move, but was soft.

Afterward I whispered, "Thanks. That's the second time in my life you've made everything seem different."

"What?" she whispered back, but I could not repeat that and she did not ask again.

10.

SHE DID NOT WANT TO STAY and did not want me to get up. She put her things back on without light, muttered, "Thanks for the dinner," and was gone.

What a strange business. A night in Chicago when she was fifteen or sixteen, chastely but intimate in a different way, and now this, eleven years later. I did not know what that darkness and immobility had meant, it was like something out of a French novel. I thought it showed she took these things very seriously and that flattered me. I had badly needed some flattery.

I was awake at the first light and my apartment which as a rule looked repulsive to me, seemed more human. It was nice to lie in the bed where she had been and I sniffed the pillow for a trace of her. I was pleased with the two coffee cups still on the table. I felt more pleased with myself (or perhaps, less displeased) than I had been since that Dear-John evening with my wife.

Jean had a lesson that morning and for the first time she came to my office afterward. She was friendly but not in a very personal way; she made me self-conscious.

Joseph had told her she could soon solo, the next sunny and calm day. "He said to get a student pilot certificate," she told me. "He said you have the forms."

"Yes, I do." And softly, because a man was sitting in the waiting room, "Will it be tricky? I mean with your new name?"

"It shouldn't, I have a driver's license in the name of Beatrix Orme. They won't ask anything more than that, will they?"

"No. The only other thing you need is a medical certificate."

She frowned, and stared past me.

"There isn't anything wrong with you, is there? You look the picture of health this morning."

She hesitated. "I've been very sick," she said. "Not long ago. But I'm fine right now."

"Nothing to do with your heart, had it?"

"No. Nothing like that."

"You'll be okay then. Heart and epilepsy, and diabetes, those are the things that worry them, they don't want you to black out up there. All a student needs is the third-class certificate. Do you have a doctor?"

"No. Not here."

"You can go to an FAA examiner. Federal Aviation Administration."

"Yes. I'd prefer that."

"I'll set it up for you. Leave it to old David from Chicago."

I tried a smile on her but she did not respond. I did not see her for some days then, though we talked on the telephone. I asked her for a drink or for dinner, but she said she just couldn't, she wasn't free. I questioned myself; what had I done to annoy her so quickly? Saying "Leave it to old David"? How could I have been so coy? I tried writing her a funny note, but it did not come off. A feeling of inadequacy toward her crept over me.

Then I got a call from the FAA medical examiner. "It is about Mrs. Beatrix Orme," he said. "I'm mailing you the third-class certificate today, but it is marked 'Valid for six months only.' I want you people to keep an eye on that. Make sure she gets back to me before it runs out if she's flying solo. You get that?"

"Well, yes, doctor," I said. "I get it. But why? Aren't they always for twenty-four months? What's wrong with her?"

"That's not something I can discuss without the patient's permission. Just remember to keep an eye out for those deadlines."

When I gave Jean the student pilot certificate, I had to tell her what the doctor had said. She had a little smile in reaction and said, "Yes, I know. Nothing terribly important."

She left and I think I was, cowardly, almost relieved that she hadn't wanted to tell me about it.

Quite a while later, when I had finished the book I had been reading, I got up to file the duplicate of her certificate and when I looked out of the office window, I saw that her car was still in the parking lot. I could not be certain through the dirty windowpane, but I thought I saw her sitting in it.

I walked out of the front door and around the building. She was in the car with her arms on the steering wheel and her head on her arms. I went over and opened the door on the driver's side.

She looked up at me, tears streaking her face. Just like in Haymarket Square. I did not ask anything. She moved over and I got in and drove us away.

11.

WE DID NOT SPEAK. She wiped her eyes with her sleeve and looked away from me out of the window.

I drove to my apartment, I did not know where else to go. It was twilight by the time we got there. We sat in the car, I opened my mouth a number of times but whatever I planned to say or ask seemed inane.

Then she murmured, "The days are getting shorter."

"Yes."

It was a kind of acknowledgement that I had done right in taking her there. She had a little car, a Fiat I think, and I managed to squeeze it in between a hydrant space and a truck, and went around to open the car door for her.

Upstairs the late light of the autumn day had remained behind in my room: my windows overlooked the empty space of a building lot. I did not turn on the lamp but made us coffee. We sat down silently with our cups. After a while she stood up, put her cup down, and said, "I'll show you."

She took off her raincoat and let it fall on the floor, and then her sweater and skirt. She virtually tore off her shoes and her underwear. Then she stood still and looked out at the building site, from which we could hear the shouts and screams of children.

Jean's body. That glowing and shiny highschool-girl body I had never seen but imagined. This Jean was mutilated, scarred in a bad way.

After a time, in the silence of that room, a silence deeper because it was cut by those screams from outside, she turned her face to me. "I've had five operations," she said. "Or maybe six. I lost count." And she laughed a short laugh.

I went over to her and put my arms around her. "It's not fair, is it?" she asked, not of me but of the window or the empty space beyond it. "Is it? Is it?"

She stood motionless and as I did not stir either, she finally freed herself and picked up her clothes. I thought, I wish I had wanted to caress her, to make love to her. But I didn't.

She had gone into my bathroom and came out dressed and with her raincoat on, her hair pinned up. (She never wore any visible makeup: she had a beautifully clear face.)

I said, "Jean—tell me what happened."

"No, let's not talk about it."

"Are you—are you okay now?"

"No," she said.

It was dark in the room.

"Don't go away." I took off her raincoat and she let me.

I turned on the lights. "Well, Jeanie, you have to stay," I said, "I need you to drive me to the school tomorrow morning."

She laughed then, a real laugh. "So I do," she said. "That's terrible."

"I can sleep on the floor."

"No. I'll sleep on the floor."

"Maybe you can bear having me in the bed," I said.

"Why not."

That night began badly for me. I couldn't get it out of my mind how she had looked standing at the window in the blueish twilight—not really the scars even, but the way she had stood there as if the victim of some namelessly cruel torture. I did not know how to act. But once in bed with me, Jean was very tender and when I was, finally, in her, she suddenly felt wildly passionate. I began to say something about love and Chicago but she muttered, "Just focus on my belly."

I woke up in the dark and listened to her breathing. I pushed the covers away and started kissing her body, over her vague and half-awake protestations first but I felt her come; "Come in me, do it again," she whispered. When it got light, I went to sit in my chair and waited for her to wake up too.

I made coffee and toast while she sat up in bed with her pocketbook and a glass of water, and I could not help seeing all the tablets she took, big and nasty-looking things in different colors, although she turned away from me.

"No, I don't want to move in with you," she said as we were driving to the flying school in the early morning. She had brought it up herself. She said she'd like to, but it was impossible, "Impossible for at least two big reasons."

And when I did not question her what these were but just smiled at her, she smiled back. She looked grateful for my not pursuing it. It was heartbreaking how vulnerable and pathetic she looked then.

"It's not another man," she added. "I'm as little a Missus as I am a Beatrix or an Orme."

"One day you'll tell me about yourself," I said.

She shook her head without taking her eyes off the traffic; she was driving and we were turning into Merrick Road. She said, "Believe you me, you wouldn't want me to."

My office door stood open as I had left it, but nobody had stolen my electric heater or the Coke machine or the dirty towel in the washroom.

12.

I WAS BORN in the month the Germans invaded Russia, June 1941. For a long time I thought that I remembered events from the Second World War which actually must have been told to me much later: "events" in quotes, things such as that there was no sugar in any store in Danbury. The war itself played no role in my life because it played no role in my mother's life. She was already divorced then and my father was in his fifties. There were no men around. My mother lived with me in West Redding, a bleak and lonely little town in Connecticut. I have an image of Sunday afternoons so still and endless that as I stood at the window of our sitting room, watching the empty road, I thought my heart would break.

As a boy, the great war to me (as to my mother) was the First World War. My grandfather, my mother's father, had volunteered right in April 1917, and my mother often told me about that with great pleasure. It came as a very satisfactory surprise to me when I read in a schoolbook that the people who were in it, had called it what I called it to myself, the Great War, and when I realized how absolute they had felt about it. They were certain no one would ever again go through what they were going through. There was a kind of painful beauty in that. Like the Last Days of Pompeii.

I knew about the uniforms the Germans and the British and the Americans had worn on D-Day in 1944, and that on the evening before Pearl Harbor all American sailors were dancing or drunk, and that a major in the SS had been called a Standard Fuehrer or a name like that. But it was movie knowledge. The Great War was the war of my family and it was the last in a line.

This was of course before Vietnam, when the American Army lost its innocent grandeur for me.

Later, the Great War kept its spell. I could look for hours at photographs from it. I imagined I experienced a kind of nostalgia for that time a generation before I was born. Pictures lived in my mind of English soldiers, little fellows in their saucer helmets marching down village streets with French children crying after them, "Tommy! Tommy!" I got that from the photographs, I knew, but I could hear the cries. Lieutenants on leave from the front drove to Paris in those marvelous open automobiles they built then. I saw them pull up in the first town they'd come to which had not been bombed, ask for the best hotel, and get themselves a hamper packed with paté and champagne. I was sure they had been happy, happier than I was. Even in the middle of that violence, things made more sense to them, even dying did. They had been less tired, they had had more guts than the grown-ups around me.

I did not know how I could feel close to lives which had

never touched mine. I am thinking of time, of time spans, links within time between lives. About the intensity of being alive for an officer of twenty driving down a Paris boulevard in an open car, in the summer of the year 1917. In spite or maybe even because of the idea of death somewhere behind his every thought. The resonance of that intensity is still in the air. I believe so, anyway.

Nothing mystical about this: there are human links. That old man sitting on a Paris bench has, long ago, seen the automobile with the lieutenant go by. Here is a link already. Who knows but that the old man remembers few things from his entire eighty years' existence as clearly as a summer afternoon when as a boy he was promenading along a Paris boulevard, in a confused eagerness for the coming autumn when he would be drafted too (and yet dreading it), glancing at girls and women but miserably ignored by them? He'd tug at his suit with its stupid sleeves which were too short. (Now, sixty years later, he still wears a jacket with sleeves which are too short. His life has gone by and he has not been able to remedy it). That automobile slowly passed him. The American officer's eyes rested on the boy for one moment, the arrogant, almost colorless blue eyes of a demigod, at his side on the front seat a young woman in a big white hat, the car, black and nickel, a Hispano-Suiza (the boy collected the pins and badges which car manufacturers gave out). How he had felt he was touching a world of unimaginable glory and joy. How he had assuaged his burning jealousy with the idea that the officer might not have another week to live. He had been ashamed of that thought, superstitiously perhaps (it might rebound on him) and had followed it by muttering a Paternoster for the lieutenant.

Had the officer nevertheless really died within the week? He or another one like him, how is one to know the difference? Many of those dead were not recognizable, they were literally shredded by the German minnies. The old man is sitting there, he survived, indeed he still looks hale. Perhaps he got posted to a rear echelon in that deadly winter of 1917 because at his army medical, no matter how hasty they were, they still could not miss the tuberculosis he had, like so many city children. Presently though, he will be dead too. Then the sixty-odd years he has had extra over the lieutenant from Boston will be but nothing.

In my garage apartment, only since Jean, all this has come to the surface of my mind again, in half-dreams, the half-dreams before dawn. I would wake up and think for one moment that I had got hold of a secret, the secret answer to the fear of death.

13.

JEAN DID HER FIRST SOLO shortly afterward. It was a blustery day with dark clouds, but Joseph let her go up all the same. "If I had crashed in the jungle, I'd trust myself to that one to fly me out," he said to me. "Some never get the feel. She's got it."

"She's a brave girl," I said.

He looked surprised. "Brave? That's not it, the idea of getting killed never enters her head."

She landed fine against the gusty winds and when she came over to us her eyes were shining. I had not seen her face that strong and it was a shock, it showed how she must have looked before she got ill.

Joseph, who had never before shown interest in anything going on at Seataugh, pumped her hand. "Five more hours," he said, "maybe less! Including VFR navigation. Then you can go up in the Arrow Four and you'll be good and ready for the three-point cross-country."

To our surprise, the spark went out of her at those words and she frowned. "Hurrah," she said lamely. "Can I treat you two to coffee?"

"I've got another customer right now," Joseph answered, "and he should have stuck with his Volkswagen. I'll see you tomorrow."

So she and I went to the canteen and I got our coffee. When I came back to the table, Jean looked worse. Her face was ashen and I thought she was going to faint.

"Jean, what is it?" I asked. "What do you need? Tell me."

She did not answer and I went back to the counter, wet my handkerchief, and got a glass of water. When I came back with them, she pushed them away so violently that she knocked the glass out of my hand.

At that, some of the color came back into her face. "I'm sorry," she said. "Let me. Please."

She wiped up the water with her placemat and put the pieces of glass in the ashtray. She sat down, looked out of the window, and drank her coffee. Finally she turned her eyes on me. "I'm okay," she told me. "Again, sorry."

"Oh screw that, Jean—"

She held a finger against her mouth to stop me.

"It's the passage of time," she said softly. "That's what gets me. All of a sudden, it's all going so fast. Five more hours, Joseph said."

She put her cup down, closed her eyes at me for a second the way she did to say thank you, and was gone.

14.

I HAD A DATE that evening, of long standing. Around Labor Day, in my pre-Jean days, a businessman had come in for a trial lesson and had parked his companion in my office. First she sat in the waiting room leafing through the magazines, but then she came in and said she wanted to know more about flying. She herself did most of the talking, though. When she left, she said, "I'll be back in New York around October fifteenth, just for a visit, I live in Florida. Want me to come and pick you up for a drink? I would like to know more about this," waving a hand at my shabby desk with all those forms and then at the sky outside.

"Well, yes, sure," I said. She was spooky but I was mesmerized by her tan.

I did not even know her name and I had written "Drinks, Ms. Florida" for October 15 on the reservation pad. I do not remember whether I hoped she would or would not show up.

She did, she drove in late afternoon, did not get out of her car, and started honking her horn. I hate people who do that and went out to tell her I could not get away right then. But she just lowered her window, electrically, and said, "Hi stranger. Drinks on the house. Follow me." Her tan was even deeper than last time, so I went to lock the office and did as I was told.

She pulled in at the first posh-looking bar on Merrick Road, again with very much horn honking, and I followed back in.

"Florida must be a noisy place," I said when we had been seated at a corner table in the bar, which was empty.

She gave me a glassy stare and asked, "You drink Bloody Marys?" I nodded. "Two," she said to the waitress.

"Not when I'm not there," she then said.

"What?"

"Not when I'm not there. A noisy place."

We drank a large number of Bloody Marys without getting the least high. I just got more and more annoyed with myself for being there and she seemed to relax more and more. I think we hardly said anything. When it got crowded, she decided she wanted to leave. I tried to pay with a credit card but she pushed it away and tucked some bills in the waitress's hand.

"I'm at the St. Regis," she told me. "Can you be an angel and drive me home in my car?"

"How will I get back?" I asked.

She looked blankly at me.

"Okay," I said. "If you follow me to New Lots Avenue, that's close by, I'll leave my car there. Then I can come back on the subway."

"New Lots Avenue," she repeated, as if it were the name of a village in Tibet.

That's what we did, though, and I drove her into Manhattan without getting arrested for drunken driving. At the St. Regis they said they would park the car for her. It was tasteful to make love to her, an aesthetic experience to lie on all that evenly golden skin without so much as a bathing suit mark. Then she fell asleep.

I like hotels in the very early morning, there is a feeling of adventure, of being lost in strange cities, in those empty lobbies with maybe one man vacuuming, and a night clerk sipping black coffee from a cup he keeps under the registration desk.

Outside it was getting light and a drizzle was coming down, but East 55th Street was dry; it must have started raining just then. The street was singularly still.

To my surprise I did not have to wait long for the subway train and equally surprising, it was packed. The world outside had been so empty. Like a different planet. One underneath the other.

My car was still there and I drove home feeling pleasantly tired and unshaven. The sun had come out and between buildings shone into my eyes. When I pulled up at my garage, the first thing I noticed was Jean's car parked right in front of my door, with her curled up in the back seat.

I thought she was asleep, but when I was about to tap on the glass, she sat up straight.

Instead of coming out, she rolled down the window and said, "Morning. How are you?" as if I'd been standing at her front door.

"Eh, fine. And you?"

"Fine."

15.

I MADE HER TAKE OFF her shoes and put on my bathrobe over her dress, for she was frozen. She sat up on the bed and drank a gallon of coffee.

I tried to start on an explanation or apology but could not think of anything that would sound right. "I wish I'd given you a key last time," I said.

"Who was to know. It's me who should apologize, but I'm not going to."

"Good."

"The question is, can you stand me as a paying guest for a short time? I won't be in the way. I know last time I was all snooty—"

"Please," I said, interrupting her. "Of course you can.

You must. I wanted you to. I don't know where you were before, but you'll be better here."

"I won't be in the way."

"You can't be in the way. You are the way."

She smiled bleakly. "Lao-Tsze," she said. "That's me, all right."

"That smell of gasoline—you get used to it. You'll see."

"I don't mind it," she answered. "It reminds me of planes."

"And I don't want your money. I've enough to handle things." Then I asked, "What happened?"

"Just some trouble. I had to get out of my place. I'll tell you when you get back from the school."

"Okay, tell me then. I'll be out of here in ten minutes. And you get some sleep."

"Thanks, David," she said. "You're a nice fellow. You must cancel my lesson for me. I'm just too tired. First one I miss."

"I'm sorry."

She was crawling under my bed cover with all her clothes on. "My fault," she said, "I didn't feel too good to begin with. I'll catch up tomorrow. And, eh, thanks again."

"You're welcome. And please be here when I get back. Stay in bed."

She did not answer, she was asleep.

16.

IT CAME AS NO SURPRISE to have Jean admit, yes, she was still on the run. Not or not only by having been carried over from year to year on an FBI Wanted List, but because she was "involved in a plan." She was not going to tell me what, it was better if I could always say I didn't know anything. "Nothing very dramatic, don't worry," she added.

I was sitting on the foot of the bed when she told me this, on the evening of that same day. Her clothes were in a pile on a chair, and she was huddled deep down under the covers, only her head sticking out. Nothing else in the room was touched, she had slept the whole day and she did not want any food. "It was great," she said, "I needed that."

The timing of events in my life has always been rotten. I often feel that if I'd been born one day earlier or one day later, I would have been on top of things. On this occasion I missed my chance because I was not listening properly; I think Jean was ready to tell me everything and perhaps let me help her, that evening. But when she fell silent and waited for me to ask more, I was silent too. I was too tired to respond, and I was too tired for no better reason than my night without sleep on the Florida lady.

I sat still, my eyes closed, and stroked her leg through the cover. The sunset was angry purple and made a fan of colors on the wall behind the bed. I loved her, if there is any precise meaning to that.

Even my noisy street seemed caught in a mysterious hush. Jean shifted herself to the other side of the bed. "You're as beat as I was this morning," she said. "Just come to bed."

"Will you tell me more tomorrow?" I asked.

She said yes, but did not, of course.

17.

LYING AWAKE MOTIONLESS in the night. She did not make a sound. I had a wide bed in there (my only luxury whenever I can manage it) and we just touched, I could just feel her hip and her right foot. She turned onto her side, toward the wall, and I rested my fingertips on her back. Her skin there was smooth and unhurt.

I had not lowered the blinds and whenever a car went by, unexplainable conical shapes of light slid across the ceiling and the walls. There were long pauses between them, it must have been that particular dead middle of the twenty-four hour day of Rockville Centre, Long Island, the precise low point, like the ebb tide in Oyster Bay. Say at ten minutes to four A.M. After which, life, seemingly extinguished in garbage and grime and cold neon tubes and old, old cars, stirs and slowly starts up again.

About Jean: her secret did not seem hard to guess at then. In her mind, wandering in that moment through a dream perhaps of herself as a child playing under the trees of Chagrin Falls, in that young woman's mind, a plan had been shaped which involved a plane. It surely had nothing to do with crime or money, unless it was to get money for some group or other. A group planning what? A plane for the kidnaping of someone, to help someone escape—to the U.S., from the U.S.?

I wanted to feel the working of her body through my hand on her back, I wanted to know about her physical reality.

Is she dying of cancer? What else can it be?

I was cold, I had to hug myself to stop trembling. For God's sake—had she accepted to undertake some kind of suicide mission? If that were so, I had to, had to do what? I had to dissuade her from it.

But if she is dying, if there is nothing ahead for her but bored and disgusted nurses, and administrators who come sit at your bedside smiling like priests, to discuss the payment of the bill? (I had had two weeks in Roosevelt Hospital that year.)

No. There is always hope. A dubious cliché but still, it sums it up. There is no hope for us and by the same token there is hope. Old cancers recede while young athletes break their necks in the shower room. At the end of the day it is all even-stephen. We do not know. Perhaps a role has been awaiting me, ever since the evening in the rain in Haymarket Square.

Prayer. I used to think more about all this when I was a boy of twelve or thirteen. I used to break out in a sweat alone in bed when the thought got to me of nothingness awaiting me, unending—even the word *eternal* made it too definite. I used to rattle off "Our Father's" then, neither believing nor not-believing, but getting comfort from it.

Precisely since we are mortal, what difference does it make? Why ever be afraid and why hide dying people behind screens? How surprised I had been, in that same period, junior high, at the house of a school friend whose parents were Catholics from Europe, where they said grace at the table for about an hour, everything got cold, and prayed, "Preserve us from sudden death, Oh Lord." For what could be more fortunate than sudden death?

I wished away the connection between all this, any of this, and Jean's body. A supplication.

I laid my hand on that curve where her thigh began and touched its warmth. Nothing I could do for her but touch, softly, without waking her up. No words, nothing said or done could be as comforting to her as being asleep, as any dream. She was breathing peacefully, she might be back in her own shiny body of a girl, instead of stumbling at the edge of a universe that is too dark and too large.

I was dissolving in emotions then, love, pity, I do not know, even pity for myself perhaps. I saw myself lying there as if from a great height, but I am not certain now that I was not playacting.

18.

WITHOUT THE SLIGHTEST JAR we started living together. She had had one airline bag of possessions in the trunk of her car, and that seemed to be it.

She was often away, late at night too, and always gave me what she called "an emergency number" where she could be reached; she was pleased that I did not question her or ask what emergencies there could be. She stopped being nervous when we were together. The only thing slightly less than ordinary was her meticulous care never to park her car illegally, not even for one minute. "You'd be surprised how many people have been tripped up by that," she told me.

That week we had the best of two worlds, of familiarity and newness. We felt familiar with each other, we messed around with our meals which were sometimes nice, sometimes terrible, we took turns in the bathroom and all that kind of thing like old roommates, and yet there was a high new tension between us, the tension between a woman and a man.

The first evening we were about to go to bed, she said, "Hold it, David," and then told me that my sheltering her was in no way to cramp my style about other women, and so forth. "Sure, okay, absolutely, Jeanie."

She wore old shirts of mine at night for bedwear, nothing else. They covered her body, though I did not think of them as hiding her scars and perhaps she did not either, not any more. Those shirts stopped just about an inch above her belly. I was high on that get-up.

She decided to go flying only every other day now. She told Joseph that she had to be careful with her money. I assumed that was not the real reason for she had let me know she had several thousand dollars. I thought she was slowing down events, delaying getting ready for her first cross-country flight. Perhaps she could still change her plans then, whatever they were, perhaps her life as it had now become could lead her in a different direction.

The idea never even entered her mind, of course; all I did was erode some of her certainty and determination.

I did not mean to. I was not possessive about her. I couldn't be, she was too distant to be taken for granted ever. Too strong too, I think. If she had said, "I'll be back in a year," I could have lived with that. The idea that she might be gone forever was now terrifying.

She told me, "Was I surprised seeing you behind that desk in the flying school!"

"Did you recognize me right off?"

"Of course, you looked exactly the same."

"Why surprised?" I asked.

"Just the chanciness of it." She paused. "And also, I had thought about you after Chicago, I expected you'd become, I don't know what, something dramatic."

"Well, things didn't work that way," I said.

"Sorry, David."

"I'm not sorry."

"Anyway, *you* surely did not recognize *me*. I have chan—"

"Not changed!" I shouted. "You have exactly the face of

[46]

that Haymarket child, but that afternoon there was only about one square inch of it visible, you were just a dripping lady who wanted to take up flying, in a rainstorm."

"How did you end up at Seataugh?"

What was the answer? My dropping out of college, the Vietnam War, my terrible ex-wife? Baloney, things like that happen by choice.

"Well, for one, it's not 'ending up' I hope. I'm regrouping," I replied.

"Am I asking too many questions?"

"No," I said. "To the contrary. It's nice. No one else has ever registered surprise at my job. It pays a hundred and thirty-three dollars a week. It leaves me seas of time, I like reading more than doing things, than doing most things. It's a nice, sidelines job—I was about to be an air traffic controller once, I worked at LaGuardia, but I quit. At college I've done credit courses in thermodynamics and in the nineteenth-century French novel. But air traffic is my only marketable skill. I'll go back to it eventually."

She studied my face and was about to say something, but did not.

"What?" I asked.

"Nothing. It's sure a strange combination of subjects."

"One day Air France will start literature seminars aboard the Concorde, and I'll be the man."

"David," she began, "We're—"

"What?" I asked again.

She shook her head, and we both fell silent.

There were large areas of forbidden subjects and we stayed off them with great care, as if we'd be blown up if we set foot on them.

19.

HER FIRST cross-country flight came quickly enough anyway. Joseph sent her to Holbrook Airport and back. Holbrook is in the middle of Long Island and only some twenty-five miles from our little field, but it is a very busy bit of airspace. It turned out she had already done the course on "Use of radio for VFR," which stands for Visual Flight Rules navigation, and that in about one morning. When she came back, Joseph kissed her and told her she was going to be the first woman captain of a 747.

"Tomorrow," he said, "I'm taking you up in our Arrow, the Arrow Four. If it is not booked tomorrow," he added to me.

That was part of our public relations routine; he did not know Jean did not need that. "Actually," I answered, "we haven't got it booked at any time."

The Arrow Four was often used for the obligatory three-point cross-country, where you have to make two hops, each of at least a hundred nautical miles, before you return to base. It is the big thing before you can try for your private pilot license, but we had not had a license application in a month now. The school was not exactly thriving.

Jean had told me she would not be in that evening, but when I got home in the afternoon, there she was, and she had laid the table, bought candles, and had two bottles of wine out. That sort of thing was not like her. I made some stupid joke, how she must have read in *Cosmopolitan* about surprising the man in your life.

"I'm surprising myself," she said, "cooking this fucking dinner. But you're too early."

She had started to swear with great intensity. It bothered me because it lacked conviction.

"You're too early," she repeated.

"Well, it gets dark at five now, and the boss told me to close up at four. In fact, he sort of, yes and no, implied that I may be laid off, that he'd have a skeleton operation during the winter months. And it seemed clear I was not going to be the skeleton."

This bad news did not appear to displease her. "Never you mind," she told me, "for there are better things than sitting in that cold junkyard. Why is it always so cold in your office anyway?"

"That's my boss all right. The customers come in in their tweeds and their leather jackets. He told me heating that prefab would cost a thousand dollars a year. Or maybe it was a thousand dollars a month. 'Buy an electric heater,' he said. 'With all those books you shouldn't feel the cold.' Why this celebration?"

"It's not a celebration. It's to soften you up."

She gravely went through the business of lighting the candles and she even brought out red paper napkins. The wine was nice and we drank it fast; we both needed that.

"Now hear this," Jean said, "Ten days from now I'll do my three-points solo cross-country. Says Joseph."

I bent over the table and kissed her.

"Now then—" She stopped and started. "Remember when you asked, 'Can I help you?' Now you can."

I must have looked apprehensive; she had been speaking in such a low voice. She smiled. "Nothing momentous. Just cutting some red tape, some rules."

She did not go on, she said, "Coffee first. Instant, I admit, I didn't think you'd approve of having a percolator bought just for one evening."

We kept silent on that for a while.

"Tell me what you want me to do, Jean."

"Yes. *Well,* as you would say—it seems there are rules on those solos, that is, before you have your pilot license of course. You can't take passengers, obviously, but you can't take anything else either. Just the maps, weather info, and a handbag or a briefcase, nothing else. I don't know why that is, really. Seeing that you fly alone. I had no idea. I didn't know about that."

"Did that come from Joseph?"

"Yes."

"I didn't know either. Maybe it isn't in the FAA rules, maybe it's some kind of new security to stop people from making off with our planes. Anyway—so what?"

"I need a suitcase aboard."

"Why, Jean, you're flying a triangle."

"Maybe I want to change clothes."

"You're joking," I said.

Suddenly she got white with anger. I had never seen her like that.

"Oh hell," she said. "Yes, of course I'm joking. It's all a joke anyway, isn't it. The whole fucking world is a joke, and that includes this fucking dinner and this fucking *vin de table*." And she gave a swipe at a bottle with the edge of her hand which knocked it clear off the table and against the wall. Then she burst into tears, jumped up, and ran out of the apartment.

I sat awhile without moving, then I sprinkled salt on the wine stains and started clearing the table. I did not try to figure it out at all, I was floating in a mixture of sadness, tiredness, and very much wine.

Jean came back pretty quickly. "Sorry," she said.

"A suitcase," I said.

"Yes. Just papers."

"Why do they have to go in the plane?"

"They just do."

"Why can't it wait for your pilot license, when you can rent a plane and do anything you want?"

"Oh dammit," she cried. "The forty hours! The forty

hours minimum! That's two months of flying. I'd lose the whole damn advantage of having been so good. You all have been telling me I was good."

She was referring to the minimum flying time required for a pilot's license.

"And you are, Jean. You are good." Then I asked, "Will this suitcase endanger you?"

"No."

"Swear."

"I swear."

"Shouldn't I know a bit more?"

"No, why?" she asked. "No one will know you've put it there. Just for once go in before the instructors show up. There's a removable seat in the back of the Arrow Four, it's easy to put it under there."

I thought about that.

"It's for a good and fine reason," Jean said, the anger now returning in her voice. "It's for a good reason. Don't you believe in free will, David, the free will which gives us the power to change things? Not this we'll-leave-you-alone-if-you-leave-us-alone crap which is all they dish out to us? Mustn't we show we care, about what they do to us and to our world and to our children?"

Oh God. I muttered, "What are you talking about? Don't make a speech at me." Then I was sorry about those words; I thought she'd get angry again. But she did not answer.

"I have a little daughter, you know," she finally said in a very small voice, almost inaudible.

That jolted me, I'm not sure why.

"One suitcase," I repeated.

She quickly said, "You'll do it then?"

"Yes—Won't it change the trim of the plane? Won't Joseph see the balance is changed?"

She looked approving now, like a teacher who finds a pupil less dull than she had thought.

[51]

"I'll adjust it before he checks," she said. "Look." She took a book from the windowsill and waved it at me. "I read the whole damn thing while the dinner was in the oven." She tossed it on top of a salted wine stain. It was called *Pilot's Weight and Balance Handbook*.

She kissed me. "Joseph told you I was a wiz, didn't he? You know trim is adjusted during flight anyway, or do you? Now I'm going to open some more wine for us to really celebrate."

"Use a corkscrew this time," I said. "How many bottles did you get?"

She pulled out a box from beside the refrigerator. "See here. A whole fucking case."

She asked, "Have you heard of a man called Lauro de Bosis?"

"Debeau—what? French?"

"No, no. De Bosis. Two words. *B-O-S-I-S.*"

"I'm very bad with names," I said. "Who is it?"

"Never mind," she answered. "A pilot. A friend."

"Jesus, Jean, sorry I flunked the test. Just tell me about him."

She shook her head. "Never mind. Never mind!"

20.

SHE BROUGHT an old suitcase held together with string to the apartment, one evening as I was sitting with my feet up staring at television. She plunked it down in the middle of the room and stood still and looked at me.

I could not help laughing, though it was an unsettling

business. "Jeanie," I said, "I'll be a bit conspicuous bringing that thing into the hangar, it looks like the luggage of a peasant girl in an Italian movie."

"Okay, okay," she said immediately. "I'll go buy a duffel bag. I'll go right now."

"That would be an improvement. But don't go out again."

"Don't look in this suitcase."

"No."

She hesitated, I think she would have liked to take it back down with her. A block away from me was an army surplus store which stayed open at all hours, and that is where she went.

I looked at the suitcase but I did not open it.

She reappeared with a huge secondhand airman's bag, stenciled as having belonged to Technical Sgt. Aaron Livingstone. She had bought a padlock for the zipper. "I'll repack tomorrow," she stated with a kind of defiance.

"Jean," I said.

"What?"

"Sit here. I'm not the enemy. I don't even want to know. I don't want to worry more than I do already."

A weak smile from her.

I turned the sound off on the television set.

"When's the three-point solo?" I asked.

"Monday a week."

"I'm not in on Mondays."

"Holy suffering Jesus," Jean said. "Shit."

"Just tell him you can't, that day. Move it to Tuesday. No problem."

"Eh—no. I guess not. You're very kind, David. I hope you know I'm appreciative."

I made a face. "Appreciative—"

And then that sudden reckless gaiety came over her which was irresistible and which must have been as much part of her personality once as now her scowling and swearing.

Poor devil. Poor devils all of us. "No, more than appreciative!" she shouted. "Ready to pay you with my all!"

And she pulled me out of my chair and dragged me to the bed. She stripped off her jeans, tugging furiously to get them off over the boots she wore, and then her panties, and lay down.

We had never made love so wildly and quickly.

"Gee," she said afterward.

"All within the span of one commercial," I said.

She did not answer and I leaned on one elbow to look at her face. It had changed again, her eyes were closed.

She opened them and shrugged. "I'm sorry," she muttered. "Pay no attention. I'm not moody by nature."

"I know you're not."

"I've never come so fast. It was lovely." And then she said, "David—you know I've had it, right?"

I know I turned pale. I shook my head at her, meaning only, don't say that.

"It's a couple of months," she said. "Maybe. Don't shake your head like that. I'm okay now. So you must promise me."

"What? I asked in a low voice.

"Promise me—"

I waited.

"Oh never mind." She jumped up. "It'll all get straightened out in the fullness of time."

21.

NOW WE BECAME more and more nervous. Time got a different beat to it. It slowed down to a virtual halt, and then suddenly it started racing and I was frightened that a whole other day had gone by. There was a feeling of unreality about everything, a feeling, very specifically, "This sort of thing doesn't happen to someone like me."

I had felt that in a lesser degree after my wife had run off: "This doesn't happen to me." I assume life goes on adding more and more of such occasions, until on your deathbed if you have time and mind for such ideas, there will be a final "This cannot happen to me."

Our nervousness affected us differently. I tried to hang on to her and spend all my free time with her, in fact I often tried to make her sit with me in the office during my working hours. She was withdrawing, she became more self-enclosed as each hour crawled by—with brief breaks, in the middle of the night often, when she would wake me with a feverish embrace and kisses.

One such night, when I felt nothing but weariness, she started working on me like a harem slave and finally made me come in her mouth, something she had told me she hated. It was not even exciting; I disliked her just then. But she said in a very prim voice, "Sorry about that. I thought I'd like to know once and for all how you taste." We began to laugh; perhaps I did not really believe that she had but a few months left. If I had, how could I have felt inimical toward her? Perhaps the awareness of our mortality can become so overpowering that it chokes off love.

Perhaps people feel relief more than anything when they come from a deathbed and walk down cool, indifferent streets.

The morning after that particular night she was not there when I woke up, but she reappeared just before I had to leave for the school. As I opened the apartment door to go downstairs, she was standing on the landing with beside her a large aluminum suitcase, of the kind expensive laundries once used.

"What have you got now?" I asked, and she answered (of course), "Nothing. I'll tell you later."

She brought the suitcase to the flying school that day, although I never saw her do so. It was unusually warm, and the school, which had been languishing, had a sudden busy morning from customers making inquiries and taking the ten-dollar trial lesson my boss was advertising in *Newsday*. When I came back from the field after giving directions to one of them, I found Jean in the waiting room and the aluminum case in my office, shoved behind the filing cabinet which she had moved away from the wall. That is to say, she drew my attention to it.

"I hate to ask," she began.

If she had not had her pinched-child face that morning, I would have answered, "Then don't." I did not say anything.

"But this is one more item to go along on my three-point solo," she added.

"Oh Jean, you must be kidding. What is it?"

"I don't know myself. Does it matter?"

"Oh I guess not. I'll lose my job."

"You told me you were going to be laid off anyway," she said icily.

"I told you 'maybe.' And that's still different from being kicked out, different to the tune of twenty-six weeks unemployment pay."

"Oh—," she said with what I assumed was irony.

"But that's not even the point. I don't want you to— What *is* in it?"

I went over to the case.

"Don't!" she cried. "Don't you open that. If you don't want to do it, don't. You have got no right to open it. It's locked anyway."

"Well, you open it."

"I don't have the key. I'm just the messenger."

"Oh Jean," I said.

"Forget about it. I'll think of something else. You're no Nathan Hale, sorry you've only one fucking job to lose for your country, right?"

"Right."

But we both knew her own lost life was an unanswerable argument, which because it was unanswerable she would never come near using. Not even in her thoughts, I think. So I could not do anything but push the filing cabinet back and say, "Okay, Jean, I'll try. It'll probably be a screw-up, I haven't got a clue how to go about this."

She went through one of her hundred-and-eighty-degree turns of mood. "You'll manage! You're the brightest man in the world, if only you knew!"

22.

THAT WEEKEND it rained so hard and unremittingly I did not even have to check in. It started raining on Saturday before daybreak: the sound woke me and I slid out of bed and went over to peer through the venetian blind. Great sheets of rain swept across the street, the craters on the building site were already filling.

A lonely car raced by in a curved V of spray. Nothing else stirred.

I craned my neck to look up at the eastern sky which is where the wind came from. The sky was white there, a luminous white more threatening than gray, and all colors stood out starkly under it.

It looked a sky of floods and disasters, but it pleased me; I padded back to bed, put my arms around Jean who was half-awake and whispered, "No flying. No school. The Deluge has started."

"Hurrah," she muttered. "Forty days of fucking."

We clung to that rain as if it were a divine reprieve. I did not know it was just that.

Sunday evening, as we were having one of our happiest dinners, more frozen Stouffer's casseroles she had run out to buy, from one second to the next the glow went out of her face. "What—?" I began but already had my answer. The rain had stopped.

That evening had an orange sunset. On Monday, my day off, the sky was broken, a cold wintery blue interspersed with clouds. She telephoned Joseph and he said the forecast was good and her flight was on for the following day. They had a long conversation. I was still in bed.

Afterward she came to sit at my feet and told me, "He asked if I wanted half an hour today, to keep in shape. He said, 'You don't want to get rusty with all that rain.' And when I said, 'No,' he said, 'It's on the house.' "

"Oh boy, that would have been his private treat. Our boss doesn't go for such niceties."

"I know," she answered. "Poor Joseph, he must have thought I said no because I had run out of money."

"Are you going?"

"No. I'm staying with you. I'm not rusty. I can fly that plane all right."

"What were you and he arguing about?"

"My choice for the triangle, for the route. He balked at first, then he said okay."

"Oh." I did not dare ask more.

"He thought I had picked a bit of airspace that's too busy," she then added.

I looked uneasily at her. There had been a catch to her voice. Suddenly I had the frightening idea that I understood it all, that she had a plan to crash into the White House.

I vaguely remembered some man had tried to do that once as a gesture of protest. All he would have achieved was to set fire to Nixon's or Carter's attic. With an effort at casualness I asked, "Are you going down the delta?" (which is what we at the school called the New York-Philadelphia-D.C. area).

"Oh no," Jean said. "Nothing like that. Northeast by east and then due west. First Providence, and then Wilkes-Barre."

"Is Wilkes-Barre far enough?"

"One hundred and one nautical miles from here. Precisely."

She or someone had it all figured out. "And that case and that duffel bag have to come along?" I asked.

"Yes."

"But won't come back?"

"No."

"Why can't they be taken by car?"

"Are you going to start that all over again?" she asked, standing up.

I got hold of her hand and pulled her down. "No. I'm not. Come back to bed. Please."

23.

THAT WAS THE EDGE. After, just before, when things are not irrevocable yet. When things seem not to be irrevocable yet.

One of my premarital friends, a man running a bookstore on Madison Avenue, had liked to state how screwing was screwing was screwing, and how you should never trust talk of values, unbodily ones, attached to making love. But our love making had all kinds of values and meanings. She, from within that beat-up body, made me feel inadequate, no, *almost* inadequate. She made me feel I had to pull myself together and be as strong as she was. She made me feel guilty about my sloppy past.

I think we were purely, painfully, honest with each other and with ourselves, those moments afterward, naked twice over (she with one of my shirts on), when I was lying on top of her but softly, making myself light by leaning on my arms, and looked into those wide-open gray or blue eyes (their color changed with the light). She did not talk about herself and yet, she held nothing back.

I realized later how easily she could have stayed in a hotel or a furnished apartment; she did not need my gasoline dump. And as for the duffel bag and the aluminum case, when she came to me first, she had not known those flight rules, that had not been a motive. (I had had students show up with wives and children, thinking they could bring them along for the ride; people didn't know how controlled everything in aviation was.)

And me? "I'll lose my job." What a stupid thing that had been to say to her. I would not forgive myself for it.

24.

ON TUESDAY MORNING I left the apartment before seven. Jean's takeoff was for ten o'clock and she wanted to go in her own car. She didn't want to have to hang around, she said.

She was calm and remote, and I said, Sure, I understood.

The duffel bag was in my back seat, and off I went. The sky was a greenish blue, a spring color, and I discovered there was no wind. She was lucky, I thought.

At Seataugh not a soul stirred. I drove to my office to pick up the aluminum case, and when I pulled at it, I first believed it was stuck behind the filing cabinet: it was that heavy to move. I shook it but there was no rattle. It was locked with a brass heavy-duty lock, one of those requiring a special key. I then dialed my apartment to tell Jean I really had to know more about this, but hung up. I carried the case to my car and when I started for the hangars, it was not quite half past seven. Midway there I stopped, got out, and put the bag and the case in my trunk.

The guard at the gate was a Republic employee. He knew me, but he dutifully studied the security card pinned to my jacket. He stuck his head into the window, something I had never seen him do, and looked at the back seat. "You're not carrying any bombs in, Mr. Lum, are you?" he asked.

"Not today," I said, and he lifted the bar. The school rented part of one hangar, and I had the key to the personnel entrance. I pulled up next to it. I could not be seen by the guard and I got out and carried the stuff inside. Our Arrow Four was sitting there, looking very spruce. Joseph would have seen to that.

It was hard to carry the heavy case aboard and there seemed no way to stow both it and the duffel bag out of sight. I decided to take the plane's back bench out altogether and I put it away in a closet in the hangar. I found some canvas and folded that neatly over the case and the bag after I had tied them down with the rear seat belts. Jean was right and there was really nothing to it after all.

Once back in my own office I saw that, the day before, two cancellations had come in. The pad was now empty until noon, except of course for Jean's flight. I wondered if I could go back again and wait for her right at the hangar. Would Joseph find it very odd if I was hanging around there, hours before Jean was due to show up? Then again, suppose he got aboard the plane by himself and discovered the luggage?

I sat in my car, starting the engine and turning it off again, I think about five times. Finally I went, in a hurry now to arrive before him. Halfway down the road I passed Jean in her car, and we both screeched to a stop and jumped out.

"The guard wouldn't let me in," she said. "Imagine that. Did you manage?"

"Yes."

"Hurrah."

"I'll get you in," I said. "Follow me."

We put the cars in the public parking lot and then walked past the gate without any challenge. "I started phoning you," I told her.

"Oh, that was you, was it? Why?"

And then I thought, why go into it again? "To make sure you wouldn't oversleep," I answered.

She gave me a little smile and said nothing.

"Well, there you are," Jean said to the Arrow Four, looking at it with her hands on her hips. "You're a beauty." And then to me, "You're a bad secret agent, you didn't close her door properly afterward." I said I had. A Republic man must have had a look inside. My arrangement with the canvas was untouched, though.

She went to work on the trim and when Joseph finally appeared it was past nine, and we were in silence sitting next to each other on a crate. I was supposed to chat with him and distract him if need be, but he was very casual about the whole affair. "Nothing to it, kid," he told her several times.

He allowed her to taxi out onto the apron and to start

[62]

warming up the engine, "We won't charge you for the extra time," he said. She looked very good up there, you could see she was in control, and some Republic mechanics who came to watch, gave her a thumbs-up sign. She was already known as our star pupil.

Then, suddenly, it was five minutes to ten and Joseph motioned her to turn on her radio. We had no control tower but she needed clearance from a controller in the central office.

Joseph and I stood quite close; he checked his watch and then he gave her an O signal with thumb and forefinger. "Okay, kid," he shouted.

I looked at Jean, who had her side window still open. Her face was chalk white. I waved at her to hold it, and over Joseph's protest I opened the cabin door and climbed in.

"Are you all right, Jeanie?" I asked.

She took her earphones off and looked very hard at me. Then she said, "I'm all right." She bent toward me and kissed me. "Off you get."

I climbed out, Joseph now gave me a tolerant smile and waved Jean off. She closed her window and taxied to the runway.

It was not far from where we were and I could still clearly see her face as she opened the throttle and the little plane shook against its brakes, and then she let the engine slow down again.

Her eyes turned toward us for a moment and I think I saw her close and open them at me, her thank-you blink. She gave full throttle and she was airborne before I had had time even to wave.

"She'll be fine," Joseph said, giving me a slap on the back.

I could not get myself away from there.

"How old are you, Joseph?" I asked.

"Forty. Well, to be honest with you, forty-four."

"How long have you been a pilot?"

"How long? All my life. I flew for Alitalia once. Lost my first-class medical. Blood pressure. Just one lousy point too high."

"You ever know a pilot called Lauro de Bosis?"

"No. Who is he?"

"Oh, never mind. I thought you might, since it sounds Italian."

"You get back to the office," Joseph said. "Someone was due at ten."

"They cancelled."

"Well, dammit. It's one of those days, is it? Oh well, what can you do? I'll call you when she's back, that should be, half past two. We'll have coffee and cherry pie to celebrate."

It was nearly twelve and I was chewing a Mars bar by way of lunch, when he telephoned and said, "Don't worry, it could be any of a dozen reasons, but Beatrix hasn't come in at Providence. Not yet."

"What? Who?" I asked, forgetting that Jean was Mrs. Beatrix Orme.

25.

HE TOLD ME there had been no radio contact at all. "Her transmitter must have gone on the blink after takeoff," he said.

"But she would have come back then."

"Oh, you know, she is a very determined lady. She'd be okay without, we have unlimited visibility."

I had driven over to his side of the field and had found

[64]

him in the controller's office, a place where I had never been. "Don't you people worry," the controller said. "There's nothing about any crash in the Northeast. This ain't the Rocky Mountains. We would have heard."

"Wouldn't she have phoned us if she had come down somewhere else?" I asked.

"All I know is," the controller said, "you never know in advance the circumstances, the particular circumstances, of a situation."

At one o'clock Seataugh put an alert on the telex. There were no sightings of her, no reports, nothing. Joseph had to go and give a lesson and left me alone in the control room. The controller had gone to lunch. I had asked him to leave the power on. "I can handle those machines," I had told him, but he said he wasn't allowed to do that. The post often wasn't manned. "This ain't Kennedy," he said as he left.

I stood there by myself, watching the silent sender and receiver, those gray metal boxes with their extinguished little warning lights and dials on zero, not even humming now, but I was calm. If she had crashed, we would have heard. I knew what had happened: she had landed at some private airstrip and vanished with her case and her duffel bag for some good reason or other. When she felt it was safe, I would hear from her.

The controller came back presently, smoking a little cigar. Then we both sat there till it got dark outside. I didn't bother with my office. There was no word, and at five he said he had to lock up.

Driving off, I sort of smiled within myself. "You're a clever duck, Jeanie dear," I said to the sky.

26.

I WAS WRONG, though.

Jean was never seen again, nor was her plane except for a fragment of one wing.

The following day, a Wednesday, we learned about a little sloop out of New London which had observed a red and white Piper in trouble, "Fluttering if you know what I mean," the skipper had told the Coast Guard. They were at great distance but they were sure they had seen that plane crash far out into Block Island Sound, at half past ten in the morning of the previous day, less than half an hour after Jean's takeoff. They had not wanted to venture out that far. They had no radio and they had never dreamed, they said, that no one else had sighted it. Maybe they had not wanted to spoil a day's fishing.

A white Piper Arrow wingtip had washed ashore on the Misquamicut State Beach at high tide.

It was three in the afternoon, Wednesday, when all this came in, after that boat had docked and the Coast Guard had telephoned the Seataugh controller.

When I was eating my candy bar, Jean was already dead, in two hundred feet of water.

27.

I SAT IN THE CANTEEN with Joseph. We did not say anything. Finally I drove into Manhattan.

I had the idea just then that if I held the steering wheel

loosely, I might be directed to some place connected with her, a place perhaps where I'd find friends of hers. I was pretty hysterical at the time. No such vibrations reached me. I set out for the Public Library to go and look up her name in *The New York Times* file; I got out of my car, stood still, got in again and drove on. I knew nothing about her and I did not want to know anything. It was too late.

I pulled up at a telephone booth and dialed the Seataugh canteen. I meant to ask Joseph a crucial question I had not even considered before: how could this have happened? What exactly made a plane "flutter" on a calm day? Had our damn boss scrimped on maintenance? They tried to find Joseph for me but did not succeed.

After that I drove around haphazardly. People shouted at me and blew their horns. I watched myself through this, almost hoping I was not quite that confused and lost, that I could pull myself together if I wanted to. But I could not. I was indeed lost.

Long after it was dark, I got back home and lay on our bed. Jean's body, now coolly washed by the ocean, saved from her disease. Lord, grant us a sudden death.

When I woke it was still night and I saw to my dismay it was only two o'clock. My throat was parched. Was drinking an act of disloyalty, finalizing so quickly the chasm between her and me?

I decided to drink the beer or the milk or whatever she had opened her last night, her Monday night. I had not looked in the icebox since. On the middle shelf stood a yellow envelope, with my name on it.

I did not ask myself what she could have written, I was aware only of the care with which she had propped up that letter. She had used various packages and cans to make sure it would not glide through the wire shelf on which it rested and to make sure I could not miss seeing it. The whole setup looked like a children's collage.

It showed her way of thinking, it showed her life. "If something can go wrong where I'm concerned," she had once told me, "it will go wrong." And at another time, "I'm one of those creatures who has to do something twice to make reasonably sure it is done once."

28.

I WILL NOT TRY and repeat all her words. I burned the letter later, simply to erase some of its sadness.

But she said in it, yes, she had cancer "about everywhere" and had got it from working as a parts assembler in a factory where fuel rods were made for a Jersey nuclear power station. Supposedly her job had not been dangerous, nor even complicated or of advanced technology. There had been no question of security clearance. Once things went wrong and she had her first operation, she couldn't sue, for she was Mrs. Beatrix Orme then. The company had accepted no responsibility but had eventually offered her twenty-five thousand dollars "in full and final settlement of all claims, from the beginning of time to the present." I am quoting this precisely, because Jean wrote how she had liked that "from the beginning of time." It was a legal phrase but it seemed so appropriate since radiation had that kind of absoluteness about it. She had accepted, there was nothing else to do.

(She had only gotten that much after a very unpleasant interview with the Chairman of the Board, a man called Dan McDonald. Why had he been willing to see her? He had once made a pass at her and given her his card with his private number, at a management-labor get-together. That had been when she had just started there. When she telephoned him, he had assumed she was finally going to accept his proposition.)

"That company was of course Alson-McDonald, and their corporate headquarters—well, you now know where *they* are. And you know the rest too," she wrote. At the time, I did not grasp the meaning of those words.

The safety rules had not even been changed and of the four women she knew at the plant who had been pregnant when she was there, three had since had miscarriages and one had had a malformed baby, labeled on the birth certificate, in Latin, as *monstrum,* and now hidden away somewhere in an institution. She had also learned that Alson-McDonald weren't really working for Oyster Creek power station or at least not as their main client, but for a Colorado defense plant, "defense between quotes," she wrote. They were making what they called dirty bombs, radiation bombs, "worse than mustard gas, worse than anything ever thought out on this earth, no?" She did not say how she knew. And she ended again with those words, "You know the rest."

And in a P.S.: "If you ever read about De Bosis, you will know why I wanted to solo in less than five hours, but he beat me." I did not understand.

And in a second P.S.: "There is more. Tune in again, watch this space." That seemed just a sad little joke.

She also spoke about herself and me in that letter.

29.

VERY EARLY in the morning Joseph telephoned me.

He said, "I could not sleep."

"How could her plane go out of control just like that?" I asked.

"Kid, I've thought of every angle. No way. Fine weather. A natural flyer."

"Well, screw 'no way,' " I said. "It happened, didn't it? You experts always tell us, no way. Maybe Jovanovich was cutting corners on maintenance?" (That was the name of our boss.)

Those words made him very angry. "I am a dumb Ity, maybe," he said, "and with high blood pressure, but I wouldn't fly at a place where there's cutting of corners. Cutting corners on paying guys like you, maybe, who sit on their ass. Not cutting corners where flying is concerned."

"Okay, okay."

"That plane was in A-one shape. It was almost new, fuckit, a couple of thousand miles." Then the anger left his voice. "Oh, I don't know. No one, nothing, is infallible."

"Okay," I said again. "Just answer this, what does 'fluttering' conjure up to you?"

"A broken steering cable. Two broken cables. I tested the controls. It's impossible."

"Impossible?"

"A hundred thousand-to-one odds."

"And a radio not working?"

"A thousand to one," Joseph answered.

"Well, Jean had both at the same time. That makes for odds of a hundred million to one."

"Jean?"

"That's what I always called her, it was my favorite name. Suppose she had taken some stuff along, heavy suitcases—"

"Why would she? It's not allowed."

"I don't know. She had family in Providence, maybe."

"It sounds like nonsense to me," Joseph said, "but even if she had—that plane has an eleven-hundred-and-fifty-pound payload. It was in perfect trim, too. Are you coming in?" he then asked.

"Well, yes. Not that I expect the folks to queue up today for a go at the Seataugh Flying School."

That afternoon an FBI man came to see me in the office. He did not act mysteriously, he showed his identification and said he was investigating our plane crash. That was really the FAA's business, of course, and I asked did they suspect foul play. "The lady involved was not using her real name," he answered. "There's a possible criminal involvement of hers on record." In other words, he was not investigating the crash as such, but the identity of the victim, "If it was who we think it was," he said, "we can close the case."

I shrugged and said I knew nothing, and he left. It. Who it was. Close your fucking case.

I drove over to see Joseph for I could not stay in the room. "Cutting corners," were the first words he spoke when he saw me. "Oh damn you," I screamed at him, "I said I was sorry, didn't I!" He stared at me, about to scream back, and then he got tears in his eyes and we hugged each other.

I swallowed, and asked him if those control cables could have been tampered with.

"We don't have too much security here," he said. "Why would we?"

"You aren't surprised at my question."

"I thought about it. A sign of the times. Who'd want to?"

"Could someone do it in such a way that they'd break after a short while?"

"That's the kind of stuff they teach us in television whodunits every fucking night, isn't it? Sure someone could." And he added after a long silence, "And she the best pilot I ever taught."

Jean's flight had been connected with Alson-McDonald whom she had been fighting in some way or other. I was about to tell Joseph about this but I did not. I thought, perhaps there is a plan still in effect, perhaps other people are working on this. I could still spoil it by talking.

I would like to write down now that I immediately decided to find out the truth, to find justice for her. But I did not decide any such thing. I felt confused, nauseated almost and fearful. Above all, I felt unreal. It was unreal.

The night long ago in Chicago was real, and so were our nights in Rockville Centre, so were the dawns in my room, the rain sweeping the building lot across the street, our watching it from the bed as it was streaking the window. But the Jean of the duffel bag, and her secret plans, were unreal. Outside my ken. Outside everyone's ken.

Even cancer is, I thought.

30.

My working life returned to its previous routine. Perversely, enlistments at the school picked up sharply. People might have seen the name of the flying school in the papers and forgotten why it was in there. Or perhaps they did not care why. In America, anything unusual works for you. Thus my days were busy.

But long after dark, after the telephone had fallen silent, I stayed in my office. I plugged in the electric heater in the waiting room, and sat there with my feet up, reading—not books but those stacks of old magazines. One evening I wrote a letter about the crash, on Seataugh stationary, pointing out the odds against a genuine accident of that kind and adding that the student in question (I did not mention her name) had been the best one the school had ever had. I made copies and sent it to the New York papers and the television networks. No one answered or published it. The insurance was paid out promptly, and the boss actually came in one day, to look around in a cheerful mood and without mentioning anything more about my being laid off.

Joseph took a job in San Diego. He only told me on his last day. We drove to a bar near the airfield, a spot nestled between the pumps of two gas stations, and drank Scotches without saying much to each other. The Scotch tasted of gasoline. We shook hands and Joseph gave me a hug. Then I drove back to the office.

I ate lunches of candy bars or takeout donuts and dinners in a Chinese restaurant or a pizza shop, or I went to eat fish in a dumpy place called King Nebtune, spelled with a *b*, which had a nice view over the bay. Afterward I'd chase up a movie I hadn't seen yet, driving all the way to Babylon or Queens for it, in theaters which looked as if they were going to be torn down the very next day. Or when I could not find anything, I would go sit in a bar. I never went back to the apartment until late in the evening.

With Joseph, my last friend had vanished, and those bars were the only places where I talked with people face to face. The Republic plant and several other local factories had night shifts at the time and the men stopped for beers on their way to work and for liquor afterward.

I talked with them about flying, and about baseball and outer space and World War Three. They led miserable lives from their appearance, looking too young when they were old and looking too old when they were young; unhappy in their skins or perhaps "uneasy" would be more precise. Once when I studied myself in the little mirror of an electric hand dryer in a washroom, I thought my own face had become indistinguishable among them, even to me. A surprising number of them were unmarried or divorced and talked about women as if they knew these only from *Playboy* or *Penthouse* photographs.

Ocassionally a couple would drift in on their way to or from a dinner out, and then the conversation would shift to mortgages and crime spreading out from Brooklyn. The man and the woman seldom seemed to like each other, but the man would keep his hand on the woman's thigh or he would touch her breast, to indicate the relationship. Once or twice I tried to pick up a woman, but the few who came to those bars alone or with a girlfriend always pointedly ignored me. Something about me put them off. Late one evening I drove all the way into Manhattan and walked up Third Avenue; at the corner of 50th Street a black kid handed out leaflets about a "sauna," price ten dollars. I went in and a heavy Puerto Rican lady jerked me off in one minute with talcum-powdered hands. I had to pay twenty-five dollars, ten was for a real sauna, they said. I didn't put up a fight. Afterward I sat in P. J. Clarke's, a place I used to come to years before when I had a job at Pan Am. They always greeted me by name then and I wondered how I could ever have been such an idiot as to be flattered by that. I recognized the barmen but they did not recognize me. I also recognized a customer standing at the bar. We were quite good friends once, although I could not think of his name. The man looked at me and I started a greeting, but his eyes moved past without recognition.

Through and behind all this, sadness weighed me down, a desolation which did not get less through the days but sharper. I felt this meant that I had loved Jean in a different way from any other love. I thought about her almost constantly, now as the high school girl from Chagrin Falls who had been so young and shiny that it was almost painful, then as the young woman with the brutalized body which had been crushed in a plane crash as if that were its natural destiny. I said to myself that she had died like a

Joan of Arc of the year 1980 but that her fate had been immeasurably more bitter because no one would ever know.

31.

I WAS SHUTTLING back and forth between Rockville Centre and Seataugh. Waiting, without quite knowing for what. I was saving up a few dollars.

Then it was late November with plastic reindeer and Santas already swaying over the shopping center parking lots. One evening I concluded it was time to face my apartment again at a normal hour, to stop this hiding away from it. Perhaps it was that even sitting in the apartment seemed easier to take than all those Yule greetings they had sprayed onto the mirrors of the bar where I was having an after-work drink.

And my place was not as inimical as I had expected. I looked in the icebox where the stuff Jean had bought was sitting unchanged and thought I'd make dinner the way we used to. No sorrow, a vague melancholy. I managed to yank open the freezing compartment, and amidst the icicles sat a card, in ink which had run: "Read this."

Oh for God's sake.

I loosened the ice with the can opener and came upon a frozen Stouffer's dinner. It had stars on it which she had drawn with marker and inside was no crabmeat or whatever but money, a role of bills. Also a typed letter from Jean. All of it was frozen stiff, like those Stone Age household goods archeologists dig up in the Siberian tundra.

Jean's note said that this was the second installment of her letter to me, she had had to do this bit by bit. I was getting the money for the good and simple reason that there was no one else to give it to: "The guys who printed my leaflets and who got us the explosive have vanished," she had written, "so do not worry about taking the money." "Do not worry" underlined three times. "I'll be damned if I use it to pay my hospital bills. . . . My little daughter is alright. She is with her father, in Paris. She is not to know anything about me." The note had been typed on the back of a printed leaflet. I was in no hurry to read the leaflet.

32.

"THE GUYS WHO PRINTED my leaflets and who got us the explosive."

I could not very well *not* read the damned—that is to say, cursed—leaflet. Well, it repeated some of the things she had written to me in that first letter except that there was little in it about herself. (How strange that she had timed this two-stage delivery with one letter in the icebox, one in the freezer, as if she could have foreseen my exact behavior.)

The leaflet declared that Alson-McDonald of Providence, R.I., was engaged in preparing nuclear radiation armaments which eventually would wipe out everyone. "They are not alone in this," it said, "but I have to begin somewhere." The world was being poisoned out of existence in a hundred different ways and all by people who thought their own motives were beyond discussion.

Now this was a boring subject and to give it some news value, the writer of these leaflets was scattering them over the town of Providence, just as the Allies had used leaflets to reach Germany. "You are as censored as Nazi Germany," she said, "and without the need for any Goebbels." That, she should have left out.

It ended, "I am crashing my plane after this into the Alson-McDonald headquarters building. It will be my way of paying for the television time and the newspaper space I need. It is a cut-rate payment, for I am already dying, from having worked in an Alson-McDonald factory." Signed "An American Woman."

What reaction would these words have caused?

How many articles even I had not seen about this, letters-to-the-editor, reports from Nobel Prize scientists—still, words falling out of the sky from a plane flown by a doomed girl was different from a piece in *The New York Times Magazine*.

But it was never put to the test. The leaflets were disintegrating on the bottom of the Atlantic. I was the only person to read one.

I did not count the money, I just looked at it. It was very much, certainly a sum like ten thousand dollars. I felt terrible sitting there with those bills, I crumpled them up and pushed them back into the freezer.

I heated up a can of soup Jean had bought. I reread the leaflet and went to bed.

When I woke up, I said out loud a name which had been hovering in my mind: Karen Silkwood. I remembered everything about her now, for there had been a protest rally on her behalf at the United Nations, and people had come into the Pan Am building, where I worked, with their petitions. Karen Silkwood, too, had been an assembler at a plant where nuclear fuel rods were made; she, too, had got cancer and she, too, had been killed, in a car crash on her way to meet a *New York Times* reporter. I had never seen a final clarification of her story in the paper.

Jean More had been like Karen Silkwood. She had not

been lost track of by the FBI during the years; they had been watching her; what they knew, Dan McDonald, the Corporation ladies' man, knew; instead of having her arrested and expose themselves to scandal, Alson-McDonald had sent someone to sabotage her plane. That was it. I suspected myself of having guessed this all along, and indeed, what else could have happened? Maybe it was "unreal," but I had been too weak to face this, and had continued in my little routine world of telephone bookings and one black coffee to take out. Now I tried to see myself with this Dan McD, pulling out the .22-long Bernardelli pistol I have (bought in a southern sports store once when I drove to Miami as a car deliverer), telling him why I was there, avenging Jean. Kill him.

Daylight crept into the room and I dressed and drove to Seataugh as always. I knew damn well I couldn't go through a scene like that; not from fear any more, I thought, but because it was, still, part of an unreal world.

Then I told myself, it's just up to me to make it more real. I must have a try at entering that world. I must begin by learning how it feels to walk through the Alson-McDonald building of Providence, R.I.

Just that. As a tourist so to speak. I have been on the White House tour as a child, well, those A-McD buildings are the real sights and monuments of our time. It is time for me to sight-see them. To see some of what Jean has seen.

33.

THE ALSON-McDONALD CORRIDORS had nothing malign about them. On the contrary, everything was so gleaming and so friendly pastel-colored, I could see how in such an environment thoughts of tritium radiation deaths just would not fit, how the man at the apex of all that glass and carpeting, Dan McDonald, was bound to feel horny by lunchtime at the latest, and to feel entitled, too, to do something about it. My entering in that building out from under a gray sky was like Alice Through the Looking-Glass. All was different.

From the sky outside, big soft flakes were dropping on Providence, or not even dropping—it was more as if they were let go hesitantly. A vast horizontal blanket of snow. On my last stretch from the main road to the building entrance, the flakes came down in double concentration, whirling around in sudden mysterious gusts of wind. They seeped down my neck and halfway met the water from my shoes coming up. The building grounds had not been designed for pedestrian arrivals.

But once through the double doors, I was in a large lobby where the light was bright but not too bright, the air pleasantly warm, the hum just recognizable Strauss-Lombardo Muzak. All discomforts of the flesh were at one stroke left behind.

In harmony with this, a glass cubicle contained a guard who greeted me with a cheerful smile. He was a black man large enough to toss me back out through the double doors with one hand, but instead he did not even frown at my drenched appearance and gave me a visitors' slip when I said I came to see about a job. He directed me to the personnel section, room 830 or some such number, and then buzzed to open a huge oaken door for me. I had planned to wander around rather than make for room 830, but the general goodwill did not extend that far. Behind the oaken door a girl in a sky-blue uniform with a golden A-McD on her left breast was waiting to conduct me to Personnel.

They had a choice of forms there, and I filled in one called Technical Staff. Presently a man came out and seated himself across from me. He said to call him Harold. "Now then, David, what kind of training have you had?" I told him I had done thermodynamics at college, which was sort of true.

"What else?" he asked.

My mind was a sudden blank as to what I had said on the form and I waved at it and muttered,"As you see—"

He gave it another glance and announced, "It so happens there are vacancies at our nuclear assembly plant in Jersey."

"Nuclear," I repeated.

"Field of the future, young man," he said (I had put down my age as twenty-nine, ten years too young). "Of the present and of future. Why, don't you believe in it?"

"Oh yes, sure," I said, "but it's dangerous work. Are there any other openings?"

"Not on the East Coast," he answered, "and on your level all our different plants hire locally. Now if you have any physics, you'll be aware that no industrial activity is without its dangers. Our statistics show that it's safer to work in our plants than to take a shower in your own bathroom."

"Gee, no more showers for me."

He focussed on me for the first time, and I gave him a boyish smile to show I was joking.

"Starting salary, one hundred and ninety-five dollars," he said.

I looked impressed, which pleased him. Sixty more than the flying school.

"That's not bad now, is it?" he said. "It's simple work."

"No. Yes. I wonder why you have vacancies."

"People, especially young people, are prejudiced against the work. All those stories put out by our bleeding-heart environmentalists—and they're the first to holler when there's a power cut and their bedroom air conditioner conks out."

We exchanged a conspiratorial smile over the bleeding hearts in their stuffy bedrooms.

He pulled an IBM card from a box. "Shall we set some wheels in motion?"

"I'd like to think it over."

He put the card back but he stayed jolly. "As you wish, David," he said. "Return your application to the receptionist, she'll file it. Call us when you've decided. Here's my direct number."

I had thought to do some wandering now, but the sky-blue girl was sitting in the reception area waiting for me.

"Any luck?" she asked in the elevator.

"Yes. I'll be an assembler, of neutron bombs."

"How nice," she said. She and all of them in that elevator were staring mesmerized at the lighted numbers coming up. There was total silence, no Muzak even. It is odd how in some buildings everyone talks in the elevators and in others, no one. Like the difference between the sound levels in Italian and German restaurants.

I went out into the slush to the stop for the bus back to the airport. Sleet was still coming down but with a long pause now after each flake. A bit of blue had become visible in the sky, far off near a horizon of chimneys and aerials.

I could see the top floor of the A-McD building from the bus stop, and next to it an Eiffel Tower kind of structure, but of cement instead of iron, and with a gold A-McD at the top like the star on a Christmas tree. I visualized Jean, in our Piper Arrow Four, coming in low, crashing into that roof and exploding in a flash of light.

The first enemy airplane in the sky of America.

I wished I'd had the chance to find out where horny Dan's office was. Chairmen usually have the top floor, I thought; Jean would have known, she had been in for that interview. Perhaps she had seen herself hurtled through a gaping hole in the roof, right in there, her blood spattering in his face. . . . The bus came, without passengers except one lady with shopping bags, its seats were cracked, the floor covered with mud and with debris as if a picnic party had just got off; I stood with one foot on the step, the driver said, "Come on, Mac."

I craned my neck, from my seat in the back, keeping my eyes on that golden A-McD until a high-rise blocked it from view.

34.

I HAD HAD TO CALL in sick in order to get to Providence and it was a Wednesday before I was back at the flying school. The morning had started clear but by eleven it was pitch-dark and then it hailed. I was relieved when I saw my boss's Lincoln loom up out of the storm, for I had a feeling he had come to fire me.

And I was right. He was going to close the school until February, and he offered to keep me on a retainer, but when he suggested fifty dollars a week, I said I preferred being fired.

"Okay with me," he said, "but you'll miss your Christmas bonus."

A bonus was very unlike him. "Do you mean the school made a profit?" I asked.

"You broke about even. But between you and me, I had a very cute crash clause on the Arrow Four. We're twenty thousand dollars to the good on that one."

"Well, a pity we didn't have more crashes."

"Don't misunderstand me, David. A terrible business. Terrible. But it's an ill wind, and so forth."

So I packed up and was back in my apartment a couple of hours after I had raced off to be at my desk in time.

I sat down in the chair near the window, my back to the street, and studied the place, while the rain was dripping from my coat onto the linoleum.

In the right-hand corner the bed, with a green cover; in front of me the sink with all my cups in it, dirty. To the left, the bathroom door. Between those two, the refrigerator.

I saw it all with unusual, almost unnatural clarity, as if for the first time, bathed in the washed midday light of the Rockville Centre sky and its reflection from the wet asphalt below.

A loop of leather or plastic was sticking out from under the bed and I could not imagine what it was. I did not want to get out of my chair, but in the end I had to know. I went over and pulled. It was Jean's airline bag with her possessions.

That, and being on my feet, got me in motion.

I telephoned the Royalton Hotel in Manhattan, where I had once lived. They said yes, they had a room for me by the month and I told them I would be over shortly.

I threw my stuff together into my two suitcases and put Jean's money from the freezer in her bag. I also took the Tang along from our night table and some other groceries she had bought for us.

Before locking up I used the telephone one more time. First, I put all the luggage outside the door, then I sat down and placed a person-to-person call to Dan McDonald in Providence. I do not know why, but I could never have done that if I had gone on staying in the apartment. I felt like committing a crime; my heart was hammering as I was waiting for the call to go through. I had no idea what I was going to say.

The operator talked to the A-McD switchboard and cut

me out. It was a while before she came back and said, "They'd like to know who is calling Mr. McDonald."

I said, "Mrs. Beatrix Orme."

Silence. Then the operator: "Mr. McDonald is in conference."

"Can you ask when he can be reached?"

Another silence. The operator: "Mr. McDonald does not want this call, not any time."

Can one refuse to take a telephone call? I was about to ask her that, but she hung up.

35.

JEAN'S POSSESSIONS did not tell me anything more about her. For several days I left my suitcases unpacked, in my bathroom at the Royalton, while her things were spread out over the desk and the chairs. I sat on the bed and studied them.

A woman's life. It was indiscreet, but I wanted to understand her better. My feeling of loss was getting worse, the move from Rockville had not helped me. I had the jar of Tang on the washstand because Jean had bought it and I could see the face she made when she drank the stuff.

She had told me everything she owned was in that bag. It was little. Levis, saddle shoes, body stockings and panties. Desert boots. Some skirts and sweaters. A very low-cut evening dress, rolled into a ball around a pair of high-heeled shoes. She would not have worn that after the operation which scarred her on the left shoulder all the way to the hollow of her arm. There was a toiletry bag with toothpaste and odds and ends. No perfume, no lipstick. Her many pills were gone; I guessed she had flushed them down my toilet that last morning as if to underline the finality of her move to herself. No Tampax or anything of the kind, "I'm way beyond that scene," she had said, that first night, when I muttered something about, was she safe, the first time we made love, two endless months ago.

She too kept a *Week-at-a-Glance*, but the pages of hers were mostly blank. A few names, but they turned out to be of neutral people, like a magazine editor to whom she had written about an article she wanted to do (she never had, he told me on the telephone), and more like that. Many dates had been torn out. "De Bosis—poetry" on the last page.

No other papers. Road maps, but nothing marked or underlined.

And photographs. A dozen photographs had been scattered between her clothes, all of the same girl, growing up from a baby in a carriage to what I thought was a four- or five-year-old. When you have no children, guessing ages is difficult. A little girl, looking wistfully into the camera.

There was no one else in the photographs, no grown-ups. In the later ones I saw a strong resemblance to Jean—and already with that hidden sadness, it seemed to me, which must have come over Jean only toward the end; after Chicago, anyway.

That, of course, would be her daughter. The pictures had no name or dates written on the back, but on some of the oldest was a photographer's stamp, "Cabinet M. Toch. Pass. Landrieu, Paris 8e."

Jean II. One day you will avenge your mother. I bought a pocket album for the photos and carried them with me.

For Jean herself had vanished from this earth, and without even leaving one picture of herself behind, it seemed—unless it would be the front-and-profile on an FBI poster which still might be hanging on a few bulletin boards in small-town post offices. The glass on the board is long gone. Whenever someone opens the door, those tattered wanted pictures whisper in the draft like dead leaves.

36.

JEAN'S MONEY, thawed out and flattened out under a couple of books in the desk drawer of my hotel room, amounted to over twenty thousand dollars. I had to do something pleasing with it, pleasing to her. I did not know what and it was important. If there had been an obvious use, she would have taken care of that herself, and I was sure she would not want "to do good" with it. The money was too malignant and angry for that; it must be what remained of the twenty-five thousand dollars with which A-McD had paid her for one tritium radiation death.

Then I had an idea for a use which would take that curse off it, perhaps even turn the curse against its source.

I was going to use the money to have the plane lifted from the bottom of the ocean or at least to have Jean brought ashore.

The Yellow Pages listed salvage companies and I called all over the place until I came upon a firm which appeared willing to bother with a private individual telephoning from a midtown hotel room. They were called Ocean Technical Services and said they could help, maybe, and why didn't I come over and see them in their offices in Weehawken, New Jersey.

It was a big, dirty place—dirty not from lack of money,

clearly, but because they were not in the type of business where you have to impress the clients. A diver's suit was set up in a corner, like a suit of armor in a castle. I found it hard to take my eyes off it. That kind of display has something inhuman to me: as a child I hated nothing more than school outings to places where they have such exhibits. Our science teacher dragged us to an industrial museum once where they showed a miner made of wax digging coal, and next to it, pictures of black lung, and I was literally sick afterward.

Anyway. A heavy, bald man listened to my story and got out a chart to look up the area. He said that the plane could be in from two hundred to maybe even a thousand feet of water. The tides would have shifted it. It would be a search, and how long depended on luck.

How much would it cost? He did some scribbling. "For the plane, anything from fifty thousand on up," he said. He eyed me and went on, "Okay. Let's forget about the plane."

"Okay?" he asked.

I nodded.

"Let's concentrate on the corpse," he said. It appeared that "an educated guess" would be eight thousand dollars plus five hundred dollars a day for one diver.

"Do you write no cure–no pay contracts?" I asked.

He pulled the same face my Roosevelt Hospital doctor made when I tried a medical term on him. "No cure–no pay is salvage tugs you're talking about," he said, "the world of salvage tugs. Looking for your fiancée's body is no treasure hunt."

I think I turned pale. "Look," he then said sort of fatherly, "why not leave the poor lady in peace? Do you know the paperwork involved, the red tape once we bring her in? I'm talking now against my own interest."

"I want to do it."

"Okay, David. It's your dough. I'll have to do some prelim work, check on those waters and so on. In a couple of days I'll have a precise estimate for you."

"Good."

"And we'll take a thousand-dollar deposit now," he added.

I had parked around the corner because my car was so shabby, and when I got there, it was gone. Not stolen, no such luck; I telephoned the police and heard, yes, it had been towed away.

I had made the telephone call from a bar. Now I sat down in the corner farthest from all those pinball and television games and started to get myself drunk.

37.

INSIDE THE CABIN of the Arrow Four Jean slowly moves her head. I look at her through the window and realize she is still strapped in her seat. I open the cabin door, which is easy, for the plane has filled up, and enter. I go forward and mutter an apology as I unbuckle her seatbelt.

She rises about two feet then, her belly and legs go higher than her head, and I gently pull her back over the pilot's seat and into the back of the cabin. Her clothes have rotted already, I tear off the bits and pieces clinging to her, and she is naked. Naked except for her shoes, desert boots, she always wore desert boots for flying.

She is beautiful now, as beautiful as she must have been before she got poisoned in the A-McD factory, for her skin has turned blue-black and the scars have vanished. Her belly is swollen, but not as much as sea stories had made me expect; perhaps because the sea is so cold here. Her belly is as of those maidens in medieval paintings.

Her hair floats freely, as long as of mermaids but not green, blond, and the hair on her belly floats upward too. Much of her face and lips is still left and she looks as if she smiles.

I know that she is dead of course; I know I must be dead too, to be under water like that. But we both still have our bodies. I tell myself, a discovery, there are stages of death, until there is nothing left of us.

I take off my own clothes, which is not easy as I bob about, the cabin door had stayed open and there are all sorts of currents and eddies now. Then I drift slowly on top of Jean, my white body against her dark blue one, I put my arms around her, I very softly enter her as if pushed by the sea and we die, finally.

38.

Usually the sky over West 44th Street reflects the gray, manmade concoctions it covers, but rarely it shines with a kind of Indian-forest light as of centuries ago.

I sat in the window sill, and then I called the bald Ocean Services man. It was the second morning after I had been to see him. I said I had decided to take his advice.

"What advice was that?" he asked.

"To leave her in peace. I'm calling it off."

He started yelling about all the trouble and all the work

they had already done for me. I said, how about returning half the deposit, and he told me to go screw myself and hung up.

I dialed him back but now the line was busy. I put on my shoes and my coat. I was going there, he could not have done that much in one day and I was not going to have Jean's money wasted.

I stood on the sidewalk in front of the hotel, and then went back up, took Jean's bag which I had already repacked with her clothes, and put her money from the drawer in it too. I picked up one of my own suitcases, my checkbook which had a two-hundred-dollar balance, and my passport, souvenir of a disastrous honeymoon in Jamaica. I carried the lot downstairs.

I had my car again, it was parked on Tenth Avenue. If all those fellows eying my progress down there could have guessed there was twenty thousand dollars in that Pan Am satchel—I went through the Lincoln Tunnel and to the salvage firm. This time I parked in front.

The bald man was there. When he saw me come in, he buzzed someone on his phone and said, "Hey, Alvin, on that Block Island job, how much preparation have you made?" He did not look at me but I could see his face and I bet the other man answered, "Nothing yet." "You sure?" my man asked. "Okay then."

He turned to me and pulled some money out of the desk drawer. "Here you are, bud," he said, "and don't ever show your face here again." It was three hundreds.

I was tempted to say, "Keep it," but settled for picking it up and saying, "And screw you too." Then I was out of the door, and drove down Route 1 to Newark Airport.

39.

IT WAS ALREADY late afternoon when I managed to get a seat on a charter to Paris. Flying east, night fell rapidly for us. With Christmas approaching, the plane was packed, but I sat at the last window in the back and could ignore all the fuss and bustle. Darkness outside, with rarely a reflection of light from the plane onto the solid cloud floor below. A sense of peace. The flight itself was a kind of abeyance—like my life since Jean's disappearance.

The little girl in those photographs was going to help. She was the proper recipient of all that money and even of Jean's saddleshoes and jeans and toothbrush, those things I had carried around with me as remnants of an unconsumated love. The only left visibility of Jean More's life and death.

I wasn't fooling myself there was anything especially dramatic in this sudden flight. It had been easy enough, standing on West 44th with nothing but a hotel room with a stained carpet and no job and no one. In my college days so many of my friends had gone to Europe, on student ships and charter flights, and I never had. Now I would see Europe. That idea bothered me; I did not want to be distracted and be a tourist.

The plane landed quite far from the terminal at the Paris airport and as the passengers traipsed after the stewardesses over the wet tarmac, the first hint of color appeared in the sky behind us. I kept my eyes on it, looking over my shoulder. It was very cold.

On the airport bus into the city I had to pay my fare with a ten-dollar bill, for which the driver refused to give change. Good, I thought, pilgrims are always robbed. I liked the idiocy, the lucidity, of that idea. To be a pilgrim.

From the bus station I started walking, my suitcase in one hand, Jean's bag in the other, first along the river quay and then up and down its narrow side streets. There were dozens of hotels but most of them had signs up saying they were full. At others everything was still dark and locked. I ended up in a lopsided place with a sign beside the entrance door announcing running water and an elevator. A yawning lady in a housecoat showed a room and said it cost a hundred francs, but when I turned around to leave, she came down all at once to sixty-five.

I sat on the bed and looked at the pictures of Jean II in the pocket photo album. I had not forgotten of course that Jean had written down that her daughter was not to know anything about her. But I thought she had asked that because it was the unselfish thing to do, and that even while writing it she had hoped I would disregard her words. I will build you a monument more durable than bronze.

40.

M Y S E A R C H was unexpectedly easy. "Pass. Landrieu" on the back of the photographs stood for Passage Landrieu, a street quite near my hotel. That same photographer, Monsieur Toch, was still there, an old man in a shop in an old street soon to be bulldozed away, judging from the boarded-up windows on each side. He made no objection at all to looking up the numbers of the pictures in his book. His English was a lot better than my French.

"The last one was taken five years ago," he said to my surprise. "Oh yes, the American, Mr. Alfred Garrison. The child came with her nanny. The child's name is Beatrix."

"You don't have an address."

"It says here, care of the American Embassy."

And at the embassy switchboard they answered yes, Alfred Garrison was a commercial attaché. "He's still there?" I asked. "What do you mean, sir, still?" the operator asked back. But his secretary gave me an appointment for the following morning without even speaking those words I so often have had addressed to me, "What is this in reference to?"

The appointment, however, turned out to be a misunderstanding. Mr. Garrison had expected me to be a Mr. Lum of the Chinese purchasing commission. After an embarrassed and low-tone telephone briefing from his secretary, he emerged from his office to talk to me himself (closing his door behind him).

He was a youngish-looking man, with wisps of thin blond hair distributed over his skull, a reddish-blond mustache, and a pinstripe with vest, very diplomatic.

"Mr., eh, Lum," he said while still in motion toward me, "We're so sorry. When you said your name was Lum yesterday, my girl thought you were Chinese."

"Yes. She told me already. Lum is a Welsh name actually. Or Dutch perhaps."

"I'm very sorry. How can I help you?"

Strange, I thought, that Jean could have had this man, that those reddish hands had stroked her.

"Mr. Lum?"

"It's about Jean," I said.

His manner, even his appearance, changed. No more diplomatic niceness. He took my arm and led me away from the secretary; then he dropepd his hand and backed off a step. "If you are referring to Miss More," he said in a low voice, "there is nothing about her that could interest me. If she needs—"

"Her daughter—," I interrupted.

"She has no daughter. Her daughter is my daughter. Mine only. By court order. By contract."

"Did she send you?" he then asked.

"She didn't send me."

"Then why are you here, who are you?"

I said, "Never mind. The appointment was a mistake all around."

As I looked back from the doorway, I saw he had turned very red; everything about him was sort of reddish, anyway.

41.

JEAN II WAS REALLY Beatrix, then. That completed the lineage of "Mrs. Beatrix Orme." Jean had stayed very close to home in choosing her new name.

I walked over to the American School. The embassy receptionist had told me that most of the staff sent their children there, not far from the embassy building, on the other side of the Rue Faubourg St. Honoré. "It's expensive, I think," she had warned me, taking in my shirt collar and raincoat.

It seemed likely enough that that was where Garrison would have put the little girl, and if so, I should try and see her before her father had a chance to warn her off. It was eleven when I got to the place. A large yard, fenced in by a high railing, lay empty. I could hear children singing. A sign on the fence addressed itself in two languages to loiterers.

I crossed the street and studied the shop windows. Toward noon various ladies began assembling near the front door; some children came out and were met by them while a flock of others ran out into the yard holding sandwiches and lunch boxes. I crossed back to watch but did not see any child resembling the girl in Jean's pictures.

When a teacher came out into the playground, I opened the gate and went up to her. "I'm looking for Beatrix Garrison," I said in English, "I'm passing through and would like to say hello before leaving for Orly. I'm an old friend of the family."

"Miss Garrison," the teacher said. "Let me see, there she is. I'll bring her here."

I stood and waited. I saw the teacher come back from the other side of the playground and with her was not the little girl from the photographs but a young teenager.

For one second, the girl from the evening in Chicago was coming toward me. Jean, younger still. Her face, and a hidden sadness behind her smile.

My heart had stopped beating.

Then they stood still in front of me and I saw the girl was a child and not a young woman. She stared at me now.

The teacher took this in and said with some alarm, "She does not know you, sir." I hastily told the girl, "I'm David Lum. You don't know me, but I am a very old friend of your mother."

Beatrix's eyes instantly filled with tears. She did not speak.

"Can I just have a chat with her?" I asked.

"Oh yes, please, Mrs. Derkheim," the girl said.

The teacher hesitated. "Very well," she then said, "but do not leave the playground, please."

The girl put her arm in mine. "Let's walk around," she said.

"How old are you, Beatrix?"

"Ten. Almost ten. Nine."

"I had expected you to be much younger. From your pictures."

She understood immediately. "I used to send mommy a picture once a year. On my birthday. But the last years, daddy hasn't let me any more. And I don't get her letters." She was crying again.

"Tell me quickly," she said, "Did mommy send you to me? It she well?"

"Yes," I said, "yes. Listen Jean Two. I used to call you Jean Two. I've no real right to talk to you here, your father wouldn't approve."

"My mother has as much right over me as my father," she said angrily. "My mother is a hero."

"Isn't she?" she asked.

"Yes, she is. A heroine."

"Heroine," she said.

Then Mrs. Derkheim was standing in front of us. "I hate to be bureaucratic," she said, "but does the young lady's father know you are here, Mr. Lum?"

"No, not really."

"You understand my position. When there's a divorce, we must be very careful. You will say good-bye to Beatrix now."

"Good-bye, Beatrix."

She put her arms around me and kissed me on my cheek, she was that tall. "Please come back soon," she whispered.

"As soon as I can. Good-bye."

I started for the gate. "We're in the phone book," Beatrix cried after me. "Boulevard Suchet! *Su-chet.* Number nine! Nine!"

I turned and nodded, and waved.

I sat in a café and found myself thinking up schemes of kidnap. It was simply that she had looked so unhappy, that her father, erasing her mother from her life, had perpetrated one more murder on Jean. I knew nonetheless that, obviously, I wasn't going to do anything like that.

In the afternoon I composed a letter to Garrison, suggesting "a meeting with no ulterior motive but Beatrix's interest." They had something called a pneumatique at the post office, a very fast special delivery; I used that to send it to his house. It would come back to my hotel the same way one day later, with written on the address side, "Refused," though you could tell it had been opened and glued closed again.

42.

WAR. Everything in that city seems to be named for war.

The streets, the squares, and even the subway stations of Paris make a spiderweb of battles, nothing in all human history seems to have mattered as much to the Parisians as Napoleon and his campaigns and conquests. Each street sign is like a tombstone for a thousand soldiers. Like walking through the blood of Europe. It made me grateful for the numbered streets of New York. We don't want those daily baths in history. Human history is not all that great.

That was on my second day. I had left my hotel room early, I had crossed the river, and promptly lost my bearings. I was not looking around much.

La gloire they call it here. Death in battle, a not-unhappy death. Here came a subway station called Oberkampf, a little town in Germany or in Austria, maybe, and Napoleon with his ragged soldiers and nineteen-year-old lieutenants. An army of "the people." An army of the people, and beating those barons with their German arrogance right off the map. But then all those victories had been undone again. At least the Parisians had kept the name signs, you had to say that for them. Or perhaps they never knew they had lost in the end. Just and unjust wars, just and unjust violence. But if it all fitted in—if those wounded who lay screaming in the field accepted lying there, did not think it monstrous when their generals rode by, the horses carefully picking their way, setting their feet down next to bleeding stumps of legs, blown-off heads? Monstrous is what is outside our ken, that tramp on the tracks in a Chicago station who couldn't climb back up onto the platform, with the onlookers jeering, who was killed by the train coming in. A more monstrous spectacle than the hundred thousand wounded on the battlefields of those armies. Men were better off then.

Jean. Impossible not to think of her any longer. Jean had been her own army, general and sergeant, her action would have killed her first. She owned nothing but her own life. How proper that the first enemy plane in the skies of America had been flown by an American! No one else had a better right. Her thinking had been so *precise*. But it had begun and ended right there, with no change, no street sign, nothing.

I covered miles and miles that day, as people do only in foreign cities. I asked myself if Jean had lived here, if her daughter was born here. I wanted to get back to New York and wondered how Garrison would react to my letter. That made me hurriedly return to the hotel.

When I got there I was very tired. At the desk they first gave me my own letter, the one Garrison had marked "Refused," and then told me a young lady was waiting for me in the lounge. They showed me to a small room off the lobby, and there on a faded couch Beatrix sat. I wasn't as surprised as she had expected.

"Here I am," she said triumphantly.

"How on earth did you get here?"

"Wouldn't you like to know. I've been here for hours waiting."

"I've been all over this town," I said.

"Did it have to do with my mother?"

"Yes. Now tell me how you got here."

She shrugged. "Easy peasy. I found your letter this morning. I copied your address in my book. Daddy wasn't up yet."

I looked at my watch, it was past five. "This won't work," I said. "Your father is going to have me arrested as a kidnaper. Aren't you supposed to be home at this hour?"

"Oh yes," she said.

"I'm going to take you home in a taxi. It's all my fault, for stirring you up with my visit. Come on, put your coat on."

She looked at me with the angry vertical frown I had seen on Jean's face. "Stirring me up?" she repeated indignantly. "You mean you were just being curious or something?"

"No, no. As a matter of fact, you are the real reason I came to Paris. I love your mother. Very much."

"Will you help me, to talk to her? Can we phone her?"

"We'll do something. I will tell you about her in the taxi. Come on."

"If you promise I can come back to see you."

43.

I COULDN'T GO BACK to New York yet. In the taxi to her house Beatrix had done all the talking. I still had to tell her about her mother. It was going to be very bad and I decided I would take my time.

Beatrix had told me that her parents had got divorced long ago. Yes, she was born in Paris and she did not even remember her mother. All she knew was that her daddy had said that her mother belonged in prison and was never to be mentioned. But Beatrix knew her mother was a hero, heroine, because her father had been afraid when he said that." "Daddy is often afraid," she said, "but of the wrong things."

"What's the wrong things?" I had asked.

"He's not afraid of the baddies. He is afraid of the good people."

"Oh."

And when she had tried to talk about her mother all the same, like on her birthday, his anger wasn't really anger but like being scared, and he had sounded like the fat bad man in *Dallàz*. What was *Dallàz?* The television series, of course. "I know about divorce," Beatrix said. "Lots of kids in my class have it. I know about lovers too. But this with my mommy is different. If a mother marries another man, her child always stays with her. That's why I know with my mommy it is different."

I got myself a job.

It happened through the American Embassy press office or information service or whatever it is called. I went there to look up Garrison in the Foreign Service register: he turned out to be Alfred T. Garrison III, his permanent address was his mother's, some kind of French estate and presumably the reason why he could stay in France all that time. "Father deceased. Div. One dau."

I turned back through the years and was down to 1971 before Jean appeared in lieu of the "Div.": "Marr. (To the former Jean More)."

In the one before that, 1970, there was neither Jean nor, of course, "Div." She had made it in only one issue.

Beatrix had been born in 1971. Jean must have married

this man in 1970, a year or even less after her high school graduation. God help her. Instead of being nicely laid on her Grand Tour in one or two foreign languages, she had been made an honest woman in American by Garrison III with his château mother. Jean, why must you go the whole way?

Think of that mother and son pronouncing "Ohio" with pursed lips and raised eyebrows, this damn attaché with his sick-dog hair, getting a seventeen-year-old shiny Chagrin Falls virgin for a bride, probably feeling he was doing her a favor, getting her pregnant right off to make a Garrison Roman IV, and then eradicating her from his life— why? Had she fallen in love with someone else, sullied the Garrison honor? Or more likely, had the FBI discreetly contacted the Ambassador?

They had all the publications at that office about American and international agencies, and as I needed to get work and earn some money, and as foreigners are not allowed to take a French job, I looked through them. (That morning I had telephoned the *Herald Tribune* about a job and they told me every American stuck in Paris came to them. They did not even want to take my name.)

Anyway. A day later I was a temporary clerk at an office of the American Battle Monuments Commission. They are the people who look after the graves of U.S. soldiers from the two world wars.

That office was in Suresnes, in the Paris suburbs, and hard to reach without a car; I would have to get up before seven again. No one was there but a retired major, U.S. Army, and the middle-aged lady who typed his letters and made his coffee.

My job was to be for some weeks only; the major thought that the post would be either abolished or filled from the States. I was early my first morning, before nine, but he was already there. I told him immediately that I was not a veteran as I had said on the telephone the day before. "I can't think quickly enough when I'm telephoning," I said by way of explanation, and he seemed to sympathize with that. "It doesn't matter much," he assured me.

"My father served in the Seventh Army," I added to my confession. "He was killed in Italy."

I did not say that to make sure of the job. It was a lie but I often thought of my father in such ways. It was a better reality than the real one (to me, if presumably not to him).

The major, whose name was John Pitman, was frail and old, but he sounded in most of what he said like Patton in that movie. He believed in all American wars and he still believed in war, he informed me right away. NATO was a continuation of the Grand Alliance of World War II, and that war was not over.

"Sir, the alliance was to defeat Germany. NATO is half-German."

I missed the point there, he said.

He must have approved of me, though, for on that, my first day, he took me to lunch in a nearby café and while we were still over the sardines and beets hors d'oeuvres, told me his father had wanted him to be a doctor, and that at one point he had been the youngest Jewish captain in the U.S. Army. It made me smile, the double qualification I mean.

"That was nothing to smile about, fellow," he said. "In those days before Israel, Jews were supposed to make lousy soldiers. I know, Freud, Einstein. But when all is said and done, the world respects one thing only, and that is soldierliness."

He considered his own words, though he must have spoken them innumerable times before.

"And if I didn't believe that," he said, "I wouldn't be

able to do this job. My job is graves, graves of young men. It doesn't sadden me because I know what they died for. I think most of them did, too. I hope so. There are good and bad fights."

I muttered, "The battle of Oberkampf."

When we had our coffees, the major suddenly wondered aloud why I was "subdued and restless at the same time." "I haven't asked you yet what you're doing in Paris," he said but did not pause as if asking it then. "My prescription for you, young fellow," he went on, "is, you need a *grue*."

"What's a grue, Major?"

"Oh, you don't know, do you? Well, you'll have to ask someone else but me."

44.

GRUE IS FRENCH for prostitute. I looked it up in the office dictionary once I had figured out how to spell it. It sounded dated, going back to what I guessed must have been the major's wild days.

That evening I was all alone in the railroad car returning from Suresnes, for I was moving against the commuter traffic. I got off at the wrong station and once outside found myself on a deserted avenue.

It was strangely quiet, as quiet as no New York street could be at such an hour. A double line of trees did not make that scene less sad; they were bare and swaying in the high wind which rippled the drying puddles on the asphalt. The ground floors of the heavy, light-gray buildings on each side, offices presumably, were dark, but higher up in those solid walls lights shone behind curtained windows.

I imagined men and women sitting down there for their evening meals, opening wine, bringing in dishes from the kitchen. I was in the grip of a longing for I hardly knew what, for a life perhaps of going home at night to someone you liked and trusted and who liked or even loved you. A woman you weren't going to make a pass at after dinner but who'd creep in bed with you as a matter of course.

In the block ahead I saw bright light which looked like a café and I hurried to it. It turned out to be the lit windows of a store selling bathroom and plumbing fixtures, and I stood and stared at tubs and toilets in matching pastels under the fluorescence, more heavy-hearted than I had been since Providence. Then I waited awhile at a bus stop, but in the end started walking to what I assumed was the direction of the river and my hotel. I tried to march, whistling "Sound Off," and that helped.

I came to a square and across from it the streets were narrower, with people and lights. Behind plate-glass windows I saw bar counters with girls sitting in twos and threes, looking out for customers, their eyes meeting mine. I entered one of those places and ordered a beer from the barman. It was the last thing I wanted for I was frozen, but I could not quickly enough think of anything else to ask for in French.

I stood to the side holding the bottle and the glass, and a dark-haired woman with an unlit cigarette in her mouth got off her stool and asked me for a match. I said in what I think was reasonable French that I was sorry but I did not smoke and had no matches.

She took the cigarette out of her mouth and asked, "Are you looking for a woman?" "Yes," I said. "This is my program," she told me ("Voici mon programme"). "Two hundred, just like this. Four hundred, for me to take everything off." She spoke slowly now and acted this out, doubting that I understood her. "Okay," I answered. "Okay what?" "Okay, four hundred francs."

"We drink something first?" she asked.

I nodded, and she waved her glass at the barman. Only then did I study her more carefully. She looked a prosperous lady, with alligator shoes and bag. But since she was a grue all right, the enterprise had the major's blessing; even if she's a victim of society and so on, she's better off with my four hundred francs—Christ, that's a hundred dollars! I hadn't realized that. The girl, or woman, watching my face, said with careful pronunciation of each word, "You may pay with a check. If," she added, "you have a banker's card." I stared at her, and she opened her purse and showed me her banker's card, together with a bunch of other credit cards in a plastic wallet. And she looked at me so much like a Bloomingdales floor manager waiting to inspect a customer's driver's license that I put ten francs on the bar and fled.

I could not stop myself from looking in from the street. She was back at the bar and shook her head at me; to show maybe I should have known I couldn't afford it before I came in, not because she thought me rude.

But I had wanted to find places and women I knew from my books, out of Zola or Maxim Gorki or even from the faded poverty of our own Depression, put-putting down Main Street of a dusty town with a dollar for gas, a dollar for a woman, in your pocket. To lose yourself in a slum room where you would hear a child cry behind a curtain and where a Virgin Mary hung over the bed.

Perhaps those places do not exist any more.

I stood in line with a tray in a self-service restaurant but I kept turning around that idea: to lose yourself. And now even the thought that the well-dressed lady in the alligator shoes would for a hundred dollars have taken off her two-piece suit, her underwear, her stockings, for me, was hard to believe and exciting. I walked out and got into a taxi, as I had just saved myself a hundred dollars anyway.

I asked to be taken to Les Halles, which I knew from all my books to be a real red-light district with whores in all the doorways and onion soup afterward. "No more— all gone," the driver said after a while. He dropped me in the area—building sites, a muddy terrain, night watchmen in wooden cabins—and drove off before I had formulated a protest. Beyond there, as I painfully marched on, I came into a maze of dark alleyways. A few men were standing around on corners and outside little bars, men with dark southern faces against the collars of their shabby northern windbreakers and sheepskins. A very cold wind was blowing.

I came to a window where a woman was sitting in full view, bathed in a pink light. She was watching television; she wore an open dressing gown only and I could see her breasts. She wasn't very young but she looked nice. The room was just what I had imagined: tiny, a stand with a ewer and a bidet, a small black gasfire, a standing lamp with a red shade, pictures of saints and of a snowy mountain on the wall, a couch with a dirty spread, and the large and new television set towering over it. I knocked on the window and she looked up at me, just as a man in a T-shirt and pajama trousers entered the room with glasses and bottles of beer. I think she was amused at my mistake, I saw her smile before I scurried on.

45.

THE MAJOR HAD BEEN stationed in Paris once before, in the early thirties, as an aide to the military attaché. "Think of it, fellow," he said. "I had a per diem of maybe four dollars and lived like a prince, breakfast with the newspapers on a café terrace—I had learned to read them in a week—you should do something about that school French of yours." "College French," I interrupted, "and they're understanding it." "Lunches in the Bois, riding—your generation will never know how sweet life used to be. Well, sweet," he went on. "Good, you know. Style. The French officers had style then, they commanded the best army in the world and they knew it. Then, of course, with that fellow Blum—"

"Then what, sir?"

But he was not to be drawn into precise political statements. "A gentleman should speak good French, you know," he said by way of answer.

That may not sound much like General Patton (as I have claimed he did), but he returned to character by adding that with the French Army as he knew it gone, and with most waiters and whores now Greek or Algerian, soon of course there would not be anyone left for an American to speak French with. Still, he insisted on doing something for my French education by lending me his card to the central library, the Bibliothèque Nationale. That was the place for a young fellow to spend some of his free time. "Read Charles Nodier, *Scenes from Military Life*," he told me. "Even if you're in this office for only two weeks, you should have some historical perspective. Life is too short to waste time, to do things you don't understand."

I was pleased with the offer: I had awaited my first Paris weekend with apprehension. After that, worse, Christmas. I have generally hated holidays and Sundays, ever since as a child I had to see my mother cry through Christmases and New Year's Eves and have her tell me how every woman had someone except she. (She did have a boyfriend for decades, as I realized much later, but he was a married man. He used to telephone her after midnight on New Year's Eve and say, "Sorry, wrong number, but a happy New Year anyway").

They let me into the library on Saturday, though on the way over I had discovered the major's card had his photograph on it. I guess he had not thought of that. But I did not read his Charles Nodier or anything else, I just sat there, behind some books left on the table by someone else, and drew stars and crosses on pieces of scrap paper. It was a neater place than the 42nd Street library, no bums were sleeping in any chairs and no one was doing the crossword from an old newspaper, but it was even gloomier.

A troubled light was coming in from the skylights, rows of them sitting in cupolas as of a harem designed by an industrial architect. Fifty-watt bulbs or maybe twenty-five-watt ones sat in holders painted sky blue, Alson-McDonald blue. I could detect a smell of boredom or even despair, what they had called in my college French Lit. class *le spleen,* it was as distinct as the gasoline in my Rockville apartment which, I only now realized, I had left without paying the rent or telling the owner.

Obliquely across from me at the same table a girl was making notes from a book about music; she had a slim gold pencil and a pigskin notebook. Once her eyes slid over me like a lighthouse beam slides over the sea; she was protected from the poor and the hostile by her total indifference.

What on earth am I doing here. I'm too far from my own world, of which there isn't that much to begin with.

At five that afternoon I went to meet Beatrix with her American nanny or au pair. She had invited me by telephone. Her father was away for the weekend and the nanny did not mind, she had assured me. We met in a tearoom on Boulevard Haussmann; they had been shopping. The nanny was really a nurse by profession and had taken the job because she had wanted to come to Europe. She and I talked about Paris and the weak dollar and the merits of European and American schools. Beatrix suddenly seemed just a little girl in that setting, someone else's daughter, a slightly spoiled child quarreling with her nanny about the yes or no of a second cream puff. Back out on the sidewalk she told me she was going to spend Christmas on a ski holiday with her school class and said good-bye to me with a polite handshake. Then she did a little step forward and whispered, "Look in your pocket."

46.

ON SUNDAY MORNING my bedroom was suffused with sunlight when I opened my eyes. The sky was clear and the windows across the street sparkled blindingly with reflected sunrays. I sat up with my pillow propped against the wall behind me and looked at the scene, at the thin, unevenly cut window curtains which had ended up draped around the radiator, the washbasin with the bidet under it (the first day it had seemed interesting but I always hit my shins on it when I washed), the wobbly table with an easy chair, and the wardrobe which had a full-length mirror in which I could see myself, a rather long face, pale, not very appealing. I stood up in bed and saw my body, very thin, considered making myself come, saw it react to that, but let myself be distracted by other thoughts and fell back down and got under the covers.

I have no link with this city, I could vanish and die here without a ripple. In six months I will be forty. Forty! *Nel mezzo del cammin di* something or other. Halfway down the road of life. But I have done next to nothing so far with my share, my more than average share of things, of food, of books, of everything. How much time I have already wasted!

I think I would have liked to live in the old days when life was a circle of years and you died in the fullness of time, if you were not hanged or put to the sword first, of course; we run along a straight line now, toward a diminishing perspective as in a children's drawing. I always chose "long ago" in school when we played "When would you have liked to live? Who would you have liked to be?" And I picked Byron, or that corner-of-a-foreign-field English poet. I cannot think of his name, he lies buried on a Greek island, having died in the Great War.

My jacket hung over the chair beside the bed; I fished out the note Beatrix had put in my pocket in the tearoom. "I've thought and I think Jean Two sounds silly. But I don't want to be a Beatrix any longer. I will call myself Jean from now on. Not at home of course. You mustn't go away. You must help. I'm unfriendly to you today to fool Angie"—that was the nanny—"Yours sincerely, Jean."

It was written in a nice hand. *Sincerely* was spelled with an *i* in the middle instead of an *e*. A P.S. said, "You *must* answer me. When the mailman comes my daddy is still in bed."

When I saw her next, the evening before she was going on her ski outing, she told me, "I want to run away and go back to my mommy. Will you help?"

By then we had talked so much about her mother in the present tense that I had ruined the chance of simply breaking the news that her mother was dead. She mistook my uneasy silence for a lack of response. "Look," she said, "I've never shown this to anyone." She pulled out a battered little wallet she was wearing on a string around her neck. She took out a photograph and handed it to me. It was Jean, her mother, on the deck of a sailing boat. She wore a rather old-fashioned bathing suit and looked buxom and marvelous. She had a radiant smile and she looked wise, I thought, and glamorous too. In control. I turned it over. "My favorite picture," was written on the back in her handwriting. And "July 1970." Her Europe graduation–Garrison III summer.

"It's the only picture I have," Beatrix said. Then she pulled a banknote out of the wallet and put it on the table. (We were in a café around the corner from her street; she was playing hookey from her piano lesson.) It was fifty francs.

"What's that for?"

"To phone! I know it's very expensive. But you see, I have money. I want to phone her."

I said we couldn't, I didn't know where her mother was just then. I think in that second Beatrix began to suspect the truth and was afraid to insist. Her face became drawn, lines appeared in it, and she did not look like a child. "You go on your vacation trip," I said hastily. "When you come back it will all be straightened out. Don't you worry," and she accepted that.

Jean's money was already in a bank, in Beatrix's name and my own name jointly—it could not be done otherwise with a minor. I had used Beatrix's note to me, to imitate her writing in the signature "Beatrix Jean More Garrison." It was my first successful action, a reemergence of that name Jean More which they had thought to erase forever.

I know whom I mean with that "they," that is to say, I know it underneath. It is waiting to come to light in my mind. "They" are not only Dan McD, that is certain.

47.

"ARE YOU CURIOUS to see it?" the man from the graves commission asked.

Before I could think of a polite way to decline, he lifted the lid of the metal container (it was not a coffin) and showed me a corpse. It was less than a body, more than a skeleton, but it was neither frightening nor repulsive. It looked like an unwrapped mummy or the figure of an old Red Indian made of leather.

These were the remains of an American soldier killed in World War Two and discovered just that week in the Black Forest of Germany.

I was in Garches, a town halfway between our office in Suresnes, and Versailles, sent there by the major. Garches had the head office of the graves commission, "Now called the Battle Monuments Commission," the major had said, "because this is the age of the cowardly euphemisms." He had sent me to get the papers on the case of this soldier who was to be buried in "our" cemetery, the American World Wars One and Two Military Cemetery of Suresnes.

It had been a long trip to Garches without a car. As I walked up from the suburban railroad station, the gaps between the houses got larger and larger, I had to pass a golf course with ladies in fur coats and slacks, and finally came to a massive villa with the American flag flying. That was the place. I had expected an austere office not much bigger than ours, but here some thirty to forty people were working and the grounds were filled with diplomatic-license-plate cars. I would not have thought that taking care of graves from the fourth- and third-to-last war we fought was still such an enterprise.

It was all matter-of-fact, an office like any other, and why not, they did not deal in men but in remains, skin and bones, and all the to-do of crosses with "Comrade-in-Arms" inscriptions (as we had at Suresnes) and flags and reflecting pools is not for those soldiers who have disappeared (as French puts it so accurately, *qui ont disparu*— a point made by the major, this), but for mothers or wives or children. In that sense it is propaganda. It is one thing they will not be able to do after World War Three.

I had shown up in Garches just as a messenger, but the man I had been told to see seemed eager to talk with me. He must have been bored. When he opened the container, I thought first he was trying to shock me for some reason, but then realized he took pride in his job. "You know," he asked, "why now after all those years they are finding new corpses from Two and even from One?" (World Wars Two and One, that meant.) "It's because cheap metal detectors have come on the market and kids and grown-ups too are treasure hunting all over the place. In America they use them to search for lost coins on the beaches. In Germany they find bodies. This one is from Two. We can tell from the dog tags of course. We're waiting for confirmation from Washington, they're looking for next-of-kin. If they find any, I'm sure they'll agree to burial in Suresnes, they won't ask to have him shipped back. It is so long ago now, isn't it?"

As he waited for an answer, I said, "Yes, it is. Long ago."

"This one's dog tags was all that was left when our people arrived, all the metal, that is. I bet there was more, to register on the detector, a belt, a knife, perhaps even a rifle. The people who found him must have pinched all that."

I asked him how the body had remained undiscovered so long. "It could have been an inaccessible spot. Or he was buried by the Germans who killed him in the first place. Well, there you are. Here's his folder. You need a lift to the station?"

I said I'd walk, it was all downhill now.

He pointed at the folder. "He's a private. I mean, it was a private. Name to be withheld until, etcetera. You know how old he was when he got it? Nineteen. Think of it. Born in Steamboat Springs, Colorado, to get killed nineteen years later in the picturesque fucking *Schwarzwald*."

Back to Suresnes on those modern trains—two of them, I had to change—which are more like large electric buses. Above my seat an elaborate sign saying that it was reserved, in order of priority, first for "heavily mutilated" veterans, then for blind veterans, then for blind civilians, and so on down the list to pregnant women. How neat and logical the French world is. I closed my eyes and visualized a packed car with one legless veteran, another one with no arms, a blind one, arguing away over the one free seat and hitting each other with white canes and crutches and metal limbs. Then they all fell silent and watched the private from Steamboat Springs sit down. They yielded; they admitted after some legitimate hesitation that he was le plus grand mutilé.

48.

HAPPILY the Bibliothèque Nationale was closed only twice during the holidays. It was where I hid from the festivities and spent all that free time I did not want. Not because I was gloomy. I was not. I was feeling more in control and everything happening to me began to make some sense.

I was lying low because I had no money to spare and did not know anybody. Even if I'd had the money I would have felt idiotic sitting by myself in some decorated restaurant amidst couples and families. I could have taken or borrowed money from the Beatrix bank account but there was no such temptation.

I have the clearest recollection of those odd, almost-melancholy days in the huge reading room, where the few souls lost amidst the emptiness eyed each other in a kind of "oh, you too have been left out" solidarity of which I surely wanted no part. The unwelcome little smiles of my fellow readers catalyzed me into great activity and I set out to look up in the authors' and the subjects' catalogues anything and everything that had come to my mind lately, names, unanswered questions and unexplained references. I found the *Scenes from Military Life* recommended by the major, I picked a book on explosives, three books on Napoleon (there was so much about him, it would have been rude to leave him out), books on anarchists, terrorists, on Garibaldi, on the student who fired the shots at Sarajevo. I found that Lauro de Bosis, the pilot Jean had wanted to talk to me about and then did not. They had hundreds or maybe thousands of books about World War One there, on yellowed cards which had not been touched in a long time.

At the call desk, an elderly lady was on duty in a black

dress, an evening dress really, and with heavy makeup. She looked quite nice. She noticed my taking in her appearance and told me, "I wanted my neighbors to think I was off to a chic reception. I used to at Christmas," she went on, "when the general was alive."

The general. Her father? Her husband? General de Gaulle? She looked at the pile of book requests I had filled in and said, "That is very many, monsieur." "Are they too many?" I asked. "Well—there are only a few people on duty today. You will have a long wait." "An hour?" "More like two or three hours," she answered.

So I marked my seat at a table opposite her with the pad and pencil I had brought, and went out into the street. The city had the stillness of a Sunday, until, that is, I came to another of those Algerian or Arab streets I had run into before on my hundred-dollar grue night. Here the shops were open and people were queuing at shiskebab takeout windows. Porno movies and two-francs adults-only peep shows were already running with neon ads flashing, and very gaudy-looking whores in tight pants were standing in the doorways.

I had twenty francs on me, about five dollars, which was for lunch and dinner, plus my booklet of subway tickets. But then, looking at one of those girls, an awful-looking one really although young, with punk-purple hair with black roots and a green crepe blouse under a leather jacket, I felt I just had to go with her. If it was desire or lust, it was an odd kind; it was more the peculiar idea that I was floating in midair and would not land in that city until I did it. Instead of asking anything, I went up to her and put my two ten-franc notes in her hand. I turned out my pockets. "It's all I have," I said.

She thought about this. "If you're very quick," she answered. "Very, very quick."

So we went up the stairs to a room where she lay down

and pulled her jeans below her knees and pulled just one leg out of them with one hand, while giving me a french letter from the night table with the other hand. She had a fierce face from very close up and I came the moment I was in her. She was neatened up and standing with the door held open when I was still lying on the bed, slightly dizzy. "Thank you," I said. She motioned with her head for me to get out of there.

I ambled back to the library, light-headed and pleased. Those windows full of Middle East food looked delicious now that I had no money left to eat anything.

The first books had already been delivered to my seat. The evening-dress lady gave me a nice smile as I sat down and started reading.

49.

THERE IS A SENSATION I once used to call for myself "falling through time and space," and into which I let myself glide when I was lying in bed and could not sleep. I was fourteen or fifteen then.

I would think of far places and of far time and the double void between those and myself made my head spin, but in a strangely pleasant way.

To be in a caravan halting under the walls of Samarkand, a thousand years ago, to be a straggler from some army in the Thirty Years' War in a burning and deserted village, to live in hiding with a naked Indian girl after escaping from the Inquisition in Asuncion. Nuestra Señora de la Asuncion. To be lost, immeasurably far away.

Reading in the Paris library was similar. It made me feel

I had gone back to that. I had almost forgotten. I was more serious when I was fifteen years old, less stuck in daily things and in being sensible.

Or maybe it was just from sitting there on an empty stomach, and from having had the purple-haired girl at 233, Rue Saint-Denis. (I had noted the number and the name of the street. I was determined to go back there.) I thought of her face as it had looked from two inches away, those bright unfocussed eyes.

Traveling, long ago, through Egypt and Persia, buying a woman slave. Sleeping on the roof in the hot nights, and the slave would smell of herbs and lotions in the soft darkness.

I read through the day, becoming unaware of my surroundings. At six the reading room closed, and the evening-dress lady who seemed to have taken a fancy to me, came over and told me in a whisper I could stay if I wished till the building was locked, at ten.

I sat alone in the shadowy room, behind the narrow cone of light from the seat lamp. At ten I sleepwalked back to the metro station and returned to my hotel room where I stretched out on the bed and fell asleep with my clothes on. The following morning I was back at the library when the doors opened.

I was preoccupied or even obsessed with the subject of violence. It was because of Jean but I did not try to reason it out. I read about soldiers. Napoleon's soldiers marching up the Nile delta in their winter uniforms, quenching their thirst on stolen melons and having their throats cut by the peasants as they crouched behind walls to relieve their cramped bowels. The soldiers of the King of Naples hunting Garibaldi and his wife who perished in the marshes of Ravenna. The Commune of Paris, the troops who afterward shot everyone, men, women, boys, whose hands smelled of gunpowder or charcoal. I read Lauro de Bosis who indeed was—had been—an Italian and a pilot. He had flown from Marseilles to Rome in October of the year 1931 and leafletted Rome. De Bosis had lived in France as a fugitive from the police of the Duce. He had saved up money by night-clerking in a Paris hotel, then he had gone to the Riviera pretending to be an English playboy and had taken flying lessons.

He had carried four hundred thousand leaflets with him in his plane, calling on Italians to overthrow Fascism. He had scattered these as he circled low over Rome at eight o'clock on an autumn evening. He had turned west over the Mediterranean and either crashed when he ran out of gas or been shot down by an Italian Air Force fighter.

The little book relating this was called *The Story of My Death.*

Just before taking off from Marseilles, De Bosis had mailed a letter to a friend. Above the letter he had written, "The story of my death." Some of it was printed in the newspapers later (not the Italian ones, of course). In *The New York Times* it was on October 14, 1931. Four hundred thousand leaflets had weighed a hundred and seventy-five pounds. The people of Rome had not heeded them.

There was also a book of poetry by him, or it could be a verse play, called *Icaro*. This was in Italian, nicely printed, which was all I could judge, the title page in green letters. The year on the title page was 1930.

It was mysterious that a man could name a book *Icaro* one year before falling out of the sky himself.

The introduction said that De Bosis had had only five hours of solo flight before he set off for Rome. That solved the riddle of Jean's P.S., about wanting to beat him on that score.

The hotel where De Bosis had been a clerk was the Victor Emmanuel III in Rue de Ponthieu, just north of the Champs Elysées.

I read about explosives. I had not known that dynamite and TNT were old-fashioned and that there were now products such as torpex and "shaped explosives" which directed a blast of metal particles moving at a speed of 30,000 feet per second. The book stated that at such speeds the target "simply melted away."

I had wanted to learn more about bombs but I closed the book. I remembered how in a museum once I had tried to lift (until a guard told me off) a medieval weapon, consisting of a metal ball with spikes to be swung on a chain. It was called a morning star. I had found it unbelievable suddenly that people would make such a thing, that they would visualize the act of crushing a man's head with it.

50.

IN THE NAPOLEONIC BOOKS I came upon Jean-Baptiste Kléber. He was a general left behind by Napoleon to keep Egypt down, after Napoleon had rushed back to Paris. One midsummer evening a student from the university in Cairo had stabbed Kléber to death in the palace gardens where he used to walk before dinner.

The student's name was Suleiman Alepin. The year, 1800, was for the French the Year Eight of their new calendar, of the new era in the history of mankind. All the same, they had Alepin's right hand burned off and then had him impaled on a wooden stake, on which it took him three days to die. The executioner knew how to steer the wood past the crucial organs of the body.

There was Gavrilo Princip who shot and killed the wicked Austrian archduke Francis Ferdinand and who then himself took poison. The poison did not work and the Austrians could not hang him for he was a minor, a high school boy. They let him die in the Theresienstadt fortress prison instead. Twenty years later they built a concentration camp in Theresienstadt. Gavrilo is Serbian for Gabriel, the archangel and herald of good tidings.

I soon started skipping the wars and battles and diplomacies. I read of tyrants and the murderers of tyrants.

Many of the books were in English, but I managed the French. Leafing through a nineteenth-century history of the French Revolution, I came on its last page to a story by an old man who had lived right through it. This man remembered being taken to the theater by his parents when he was ten years old. It was a few days after Robespierre was guillotined.

"Men in shirtsleeves, hat in hand," the old man's story went, "were asking the theater spectators as they came out, 'A carriage, master?' I did not understand this new expression, *master* (*mon maître*), as I had never heard it. I asked my father what it meant, and he simply said, 'There has been a great change since the death of Robespierre.' "

I reread this several times. One man had succeeded in having a word, a whole concept, vanish from his language. For years, anyway. As long as he was alive.

51.

ON NEW YEAR'S EVE the library closed at three o'clock. I am not sure why I came out of there feeling so happy. I kissed the hand of the desk lady (still in the same or an identical black dress) and wished her a Happy New

Year. I stood in the courtyard and looked at the winter sky, clouds racing across, already losing its last light. People were walking by, but I lifted my hands up at the sky. "I sing of arms and the man. Men. Women." Which made me feel an idiot. It reminded me of a Fred Astaire–Ginger Rogers movie I had seen the month before in a Long Island movie house, and in which some sort of crazy Italian cries, "For the women, the kiss! For the men, the sword!" and Ginger Rogers asks, "And what for the children?"

Never mind. Arms—weapons, that is. Adventure. Or better, challenge.

I had planned to buy some food and sit out the evening in my room. I felt too good for that now. When the Austrian police asked Gavrilo Princip who he was, he told them, "I'm a Serbian hero." "Who are you, Mac?" "I'm an American hero."

I walked over to my Rue Saint-Denis. The doorway of 233 was empty, no purple hair. Oh damn, she was the only woman, person, I had been able to think of. Even the major was away (not that he would have wanted to spend a New Year's Eve with me or that it would have been very amusing if he had). I sat down on the windowsill of the shop next to 233. It was a ladies' fashions place and soon a woman came out and said I might break her window sitting like that. I moved to the next shop. It got very cold, sitting on the cement, with the wind going right through my raincoat. Never mind.

After at least an hour, there she suddenly was, standing at her post. I had not seen her arrive. I went over but she gave no sign of recognition. "Fifty francs," she announced.

"I paid twenty last time."

"What? Oh, it's you. Fifty."

"Agreed," I said. ("D'accord.")

This time, for the extra thirty, she got out of her jeans

altogether. I was a bit slower too but she looked as fierce and everything else was more or less the same.

"Will you celebrate New Year with me?" I asked while she was hitching up her pants.

"What?" She did not expect me to be able to speak real French and thus she assumed without listening that she could not understand me.

"Will you celebrate New Year with me?"

"You're kidding!"

"No, seriously."

"No!"

"Why not?"

"I'm spending it with my family, with my mother. You think I'm a gypsy?"

"Sorry," I said.

Then, amazingly, she produced a smile on that machine-like, Star Trek face framed by purple hair. "It was nice of you to ask," she said and gave me a kiss on my cheek.

That was intimate, and thus I did not feel refused, I was okay as I walked by myself down Rue Saint-Denis, eight francs left in my pocket, considering what to get for my dinner. I was not cold any more either.

I bought two fish cakes and a pear and walked all the way to the river with the paper bag. I turned right, against the traffic, to where a little park faced the Louvre. It had fences but the gate stood open.

I sat down on a stone bench and then saw under a tree a little metal and canvas chair and moved over. It was damp but warmer and softer than a stone bench. I opened my bag and took out the cakes, which were still warmish. It was not fish cake at all, there was some kind of fried vegetables in them, but it tasted fine.

All was dark around me now. Just one street lamp next to the gate, a fluorescent one which did not work properly but flickered on and off. In front of me, not more than twenty feet away, an uninterrupted cortege of cars, slowly and blindly, as if the entire empty city had turned out for one funeral.

Then somewhere a blood clot was removed, and the procession sped up from five to fifty miles an hour and roared past me like a freight train, still without the slightest gap. I was content watching this. I felt wiser than they, sitting still under a tree which shed an occasional drop from its coral-like branches, eating my victuals with my fingers. If it would not rain, I decided, I would stay right there. Some church or other was bound to be in the neighborhood and I would be able to hear it strike midnight. New Year.

It did not rain but soon I went home. My superiority over the car drivers was not all that safe. In my room I opened the window and heard the bells at midnight.

Ten minutes later I was called to the telephone. It was Beatrix. They had let her call me from the ski hostel to wish me a happy 1981.

All in all, a fine day.

52.

OBERKAMPF WAS NOT a small German town where the people triumphed over feudalism. It was the name of a French textile manufacturer. The major told me this, the first thing he said when he reappered in the office after New Year. It turned out he had taken notice of my muttering "the battle of Oberkampf" at our luncheon on the day I started work, and he had checked it out. He had been bothered by the idea that I would know of a feat of arms he had never heard of.

"Then why did they name a Paris subway station after this man?" I asked, but that he could not answer. He agreed that most names in town were military. "It bears out what I told you, only soldierliness counts, simple courage."

"Official courage, major. If you ask me, true courage remains secret."

The major surprised me by looking hurt. He almost made me feel as if I had to reassure him.

"I bet there's not one Rue Robespierre in France," I said.

"Robespierre! Fellow, what are you thinking of? A man who had heads chopped off like ears of corn!"

"Well, someone else, someone who killed a tyrant."

"The French don't kill their tyrants, they love them."

"In the library I came upon a young man, Bonnier de la Chapelle. He killed Admiral Darlan."

"I remember that," the major said. "He saved Eisenhower and the Allies from a disastrous blunder. I wonder what became of him."

"He was executed."

"Oh—still, murder remains murder, Lum. Even of a scoundrel like Darlan."

"What about the French Resistance then?"

"All right. You have a point, applicable here. And in most countries. Not in America. We don't have tyrants or Gestapos, thank God, and we don't need secret soldiers with secret courage."

I asked, "And if we did? If I could point out a genuine American tyrant to you?"

"Outside the reach of the law?"

"Yes."

"I don't think there could be such a situation. Not yet

anyway. Who knows, in ten years. I admit Europe is influencing us. Contaminating us, maybe. But if there were, for the sake of argument, yes, then I would believe in the private courage of declaring war on such a man."

"Hurrah."

He peered at me over his glasses. "Why, Lum? Are you saying our president is such a tyrant?" He did not sound amused with me.

"No sir, I'm not. As you said, it was for the sake of argument."

"Hmmm." Then he asked, "You did get those Garches papers, the body they found? Show me. I better get cracking. I have to locate a gravedigger. Our own gravedigger died a year ago."

"I'll do it."

"You don't know how difficult it is, it seems to be a vanishing profession. Don't ask me why. People aren't dying any less."

"I don't mean, find a man. I'll dig the grave, sir."

"You?" he asked.

"I've seen the body. I want to do it."

"You're a strange fellow, Lum. I thought you were one of those young men of the wishy-washy generation. Maybe you are not."

"Can I do it?"

"I don't think so. I've never inquired but I am certain it's a unionized trade. I don't want a picket line at our cemetery gate. You better get on with the files."

"Major, have you ever heard of a man called Lauro de Bosis?"

He surprised me again. "Sure, that Italian poet in the thirties. He tried to bomb Musso or something. A good man, very warlike. Why do you ask? Secret courage, eh?"

That evening after work I thought I would have a look at

that hotel where De Bosis had been night-clerking to save up money for his flying lessons. Rue de Ponthieu—I found the street easily enough but there was no Hotel Victor Emmanuel III. I walked into the only big, old hotel I had passed, called the Rond-Point I think, and asked the receptionist, "Was this place once the Victor Emmanuel Three?"

He shrugged and then looked over his shoulder into a little office where an old man was checking menus. This fellow looked back at me and nodded. "Do you remember a famous Italian poet, Lauro de Bosis?" I asked him. "He worked here once, as a night clerk."

"When was that?" the old man asked in English.

"In 1930 or 1931."

He stared at me. "You are joking," he said and turned his back on me.

The receptionist smiled. "You've offended him. Fifty years ago! He's just begun dyeing his hair."

"Oh well. Thanks anyway."

"This poet, he was famous?"

"Yes. A hero."

"Perhaps we should put up a little tablet," the receptionist suggested, pointing into the lobby.

"Absolutely."

He took a key off a rack. "I'll show you the servants' rooms. They are no longer used. But in 1930, that's where he would have lived."

We rode an elevator, and then there was still a stone staircase, leading to a corridor with a row of narrow doors, where a cold wind hit our faces. At the end of the corridor a glass door, wired over, stood propped open and gave out onto the roof. The receptionist cursed and went to close and bolt it. "They ignore what heating oil costs these days," he told me. He unlocked one of the narrow doors.

Inside the room was nothing but a large bed without mat-

tress, just wooden slats, and a breakfront with a mir-
rored door standing open. The room smelled musty but not
unpleasant. An oblong little window overlooked a zinc-
covered gutter and the white sky. The heavy traffic sounded
muffled here. The receptionist left me and I heard him
open up the next room. I sat on the bed.

Suppose this was the room of that man whose example
Jean had taken. This one or one just like it. He would have
slept here during the day of course, getting up and into the
street at, say, three in the afternoon. A nice hour, and Rue
de Ponthieu must have had more air then, smells of trees,
smells from bakeries and all that, not just cars. Not in 1930
when surely only the rich had cars here. Maybe in the
kitchen they gave De Bosis some stale croissants and he'd
have gone out to sit on a park bench, thinking of the hot
sun of Rome. On a bitter day like today he might have gone
to my Bibliotheque Nationale with its free warmth and
drafted and redrafted his leaflet, imagining that the fall of
Fascism could hinge on one lucky phrase, one overwhelm-
ing and irrefutable choice of words.

Think how poor he must have been, think of the wages
they would have paid a foreigner without papers in the
depth of the Depression. And he had to save for the role of
a playboy on the Riviera! He must have taken an hour before he would have dared spend half a franc on a coffee,
he must have felt that was cheating on his goal. And women
—girls—how tempting it must have been to tell them, "I'm
not what I seem, I'm not a night clerk with a celluloid collar and frayed cuffs, I will change history!"

53.

I HAD TWO tearoom sessions with Beatrix before we came to the truth. The nanny had adopted a policy of going shopping for herself, leaving us alone to talk, and I quickly became aware of the perspicacity of children, their nose for illogical sequences of cause and effect. I was forced to build up an imaginary life of Beatrix's mother, forced to guess what had happened after Garrison III had turned her out or (I hoped) after she had run away. I think Beatrix was aware of my uncertainty.

One afternoon, just before we expected the nanny back, she asked, "Can I have a sundae?" It was a very dark day, the street lights were already on. I was about to say that she would be going home soon and that it was too late for sundaes when she burst into tears. She cried quite uncontrollably, but without a sound, her face in her handkerchief. Then she said in the handkerchief, "My mommy is dead."

She did not look at me.

"Was she ill?" she asked. "Or did the Mafia kill her?"

"No one killed her," I said in what came out as a hoarse whisper. "She sacrificed herself. She was a soldier."

"But there's no war," Beatrix answered, her bewilderment now stronger than her sadness. "There's no war in New York."

"It's like Robin Hood, there was no war in England then either. No war with cannon and armies. There's another kind of war. Jean fought a war for children, for you really."

Beatrix hid her face in her handkerchief again. After a while she asked, "For me? But then I am now free. Aren't I?"

"Free? Well, yes."

"Then I want to go away from here," she said. "I want

to go back home with you and put flowers on mommy's monument."

She must have visualized something like the Arc de Triomphe and the tomb of the Unknown Soldier which they show there so often on television with politicians putting their flowers on it.

An unexpected word, though, "monument." She will have a monument more durable than bronze. I must look up how the original goes. That is Horace, the only thing I nearly remember from my Latin. I saw myself in that Latin class, winter days with the light outside fading, the sky over Bridgeport in a purple gleam which showed how bitter cold it was with the sun gone.

"Are you happy in your school here?" I asked.

"The school is okay."

"Your father—"

"I hate the fucker," she answered.

"Beatrix! I mean Jean!"

She began to giggle. "The head of our school is Mr. Tucker," she said and suddenly blushed scarlet. "And the boys always say, 'Mr. Tucker, I hate the—'" She stopped there.

"Anyway, you can't talk that way of your father."

"But he's not! He just married my mommy and then he divorced her again when she had me, and stole me from her."

"Yes, but—"

"Honest, David! He has nothing to do with me."

"Every child has a father."

"Everyone?"

"Yes."

"Perhaps you're my father."

"No, I'm not," I said. "I'd have liked that, but I didn't know your mother yet when you were born."

[130]

"Couldn't you adopt me?"

"No, I couldn't. Your father, Mr. Garrison, wouldn't allow it."

"Have you asked?"

"Jean, it's not the kind of thing— He doesn't even want to see me. We had a brief talk once. That was all, and—" I stopped because I could see she was not listening. She had a peculiar expression on her face; she was plotting something.

I felt bewildered, in a kind of bitter tenderness toward this child whose face so often took the expressions of Jean's. Jean had been on the way of becoming an abstraction for me, an idea almost. Now, through her daughter, she was again a physical reality. I could again remember how her body felt to my hands, how her mouth tasted. A wild and sad desire for her came over me.

One evening recently I had bought a porno magazine in Rue Saint-Denis called *Climax,* wrapped in cellophane to prevent the customers from looking without buying, expensive, twenty francs, almost five dollars. I had opened it in my room, lying on the bed, and masturbated with it, but then torn it into bits and thrown it out. It actually had not been that disgusting; in some pictures, different from the usual porno stuff, the men and women were nice-looking and smiling. One photograph was of a young man making love in the grass. You couldn't see the face of the woman he was making love to, the picture cut that off, but beside her another young woman was lying, looking very happy. One hand of the man was on her breast, that was all, but you could see where he went into the woman he was lying on. It was subtle, somehow, the impersonality of that woman's legs spread wide, that void being invaded. I had tried to think of Jean that way.

I made only three hundred and eighty francs a week at

the Suresnes office. The hotel had reduced its rate to a hundred and fifty francs a week for me, for a much smaller room. The purple-haired girl charged forty francs now, which was my food budget for two or three days.

54.

THOSE FIRST WEEKS of January the city was freezing, colder than I had ever felt it in the States, even though the thermometer in Redding or Bridgeport falls thirty degrees below that of Paris.

I had chilblains as when I was a child, and covered the bed in my hotel room with all my clothes and even the towels, on top of the two extra blankets I had wheedled out of the proprietress. Early morning I made my way to the metro through a thick fog which sat right down on the wet pavement; when we came out in the evening the air was so dank and cold that it scattered the yellow headlights of the cars and seemed to reflect the asphalt as much as the asphalt reflected the night.

In between, rarely, at midday the sky would be bright blue and a diamond sun glittered through the trees of the Avenue du President Wilson and the hedges of our cemetery.

We buried the private from Steamboat Springs. While the major and our office lady and I were waiting for the car from Garches, it was just one of those sparkling diamond middays. At last that private had a bit of luck. But then they telephoned to say there was a delay through a shortage of transport. When they finally showed up in two light army trucks, one with the coffin covered with a flag, it was after three. A curtain of gray and lightless cloud had closed in over us.

The major, our typist, and I walked over to the union-dug grave, while the trucks pulled up in the driveway above it: the cemetery covers a hillside. A young and sporty-looking clergyman who was not even wearing a coat, had been waiting in the memorial chapel and came jumping out when he heard the car engines. "There you are," the major said, and introduced us. The clergyman was the Rev. Mc-Dougherty of the C. of S. The typist and I were not sure what C. of S. meant, but we did not ask.

We stood around while some soldiers lowered the casket and then presented arms. The reverend opened his prayer-book and said in a conversational tone of voice, "Man that is born of a woman hath but a short time to live, and is full of misery!"

Indeed, the soldier had had but a very short time.

Don't mind them, don't mind them, you are my brother.

Those few minutes we stood there, the clouds descended to the tree tops and turned glaucous. I thought that from a distance our little group at the open grave must look like a scene from a horror movie. But none of the drivers in the steady stream of cars going down that avenue named after Woodrow Wilson turned his head or slowed down, and we had a hard time crossing when we wanted to go back to the office. The army personnel had already left and the reverend, too; he drove off in a beige Citroen which had been parked half on the sidewalk at the cemetery gate. He had some kind of church sticker on his windshield but they had all the same given him a parking ticket.

"C. of S. means Church of Scotland," the major told us, unasked. "The Commonwealth Graves Commission lent him to us. That private had his religion not filled in, in his file, but he had a Scottish name and so I thought it was a nice idea. It can't do any harm." I thought he sounded apologetic.

"What did his family say?" the office lady asked.

"No family. Washington has gone to great lengths but they couldn't find anyone. His parents had both died in 1946. There was no one else."

At these words, the office lady got tears in her eyes. "Excuse me," she muttered and left the room.

The major looked out of the window. "Ah—yes," he said. "C'est la guerre."

I shrugged, not for his benefit, but he must have seen it in the window. "Not a useful thing to say, Lum. I admit it."

After we had closed the office, he suggested a drink in the bar across the station. "My car is parked there," he told me. He eyed my raincoat. "Aren't you cold?"

I said no, not specially. "I've a greatcoat at home you can borrow," he said, but I declined. Then I was sorry, but the offer had embarrassed me. The coat would not have looked too good on me, anyway. I was half a head taller than he.

It was a nice bar, with wood and warm lights, not one of those plastic and fluorescence places. Perhaps it was the transition from the dark station square with its horn honkers blowing frozen exhaust fumes in our faces, perhaps it was the brandies with water the major had ordered us— but I started talking about myself. I did not spell out what had happened, I only said I was in Paris because of a little girl whose divorced mother had died, and whose father did not want the child to know her mother had ever existed, so to speak. The major listened well, but did not ask what my role in this was. He said, "If the father is a gentleman, my experience is, don't write letters, don't talk of lawyers, have an honest conversation with him."

"The man does not want to see me."

"Of course he does. Approach him openly. None of this half-humble, half-defiant mannerism of yours."

I laughed. I had not thought he had paid that much attention to me.

"Call him now," the major suggested. "Here is a phone token."

"He won't be in."

"How do you know? Don't anticipate people's movements. Try."

So I went down the spiral staircase, and looked at my face in the mirror of the toilet. The major must be right, why wouldn't people hold out their hand to each other. Man born of a woman.

I dialed Mr. A. Garrison of Boulevard Suchet and he answered the telephone.

"This is David Lum," I said

A pause. I guessed he had forgotten my name.

"You remember, the Chinese trade delegation?" I asked. Give it a light touch.

I could hear him take a deep breath. "If you bother me again," he answered, "I will take steps through the embassy. Deportation."

I came back up and the major said, "It didn't work."

"No."

"You know, I often think people aren't worth bothering with any more," he said.

55.

When I saw Beatrix next, she looked different, a girl who knew what she wanted and how she would go about it.

When the nanny had left on her shopping, she did not

order her usual soda but (with a glance at me to see if I was impressed), "Deux thés citron, s'il vous plaît." She was trying to put some new courage into me instead of the other way around.

I told her about the bank account with her mother's money in it. We wondered how she could smuggle Jean's possessions into her room, but she decided "Alfred" would end up finding the stuff and throwing it out. I was to take it back to America and keep it for her there.

With that, my mission was really over, and I should return to New York.

Alfred was not going to talk to me and indeed, why would he. I was the ghost friend of a ghost woman. His daughter must constantly remind him, as she did me, of her mother—to him, the lawbreaker who had come near to ruining his reputation. Even if Beatrix exaggerated, I knew he did act cold and embittered with her. When he was around, that is. Every weekend he went off by himself to his mother's château. But as he neither beat nor starved her, his behavior was no one else's business.

Beatrix did not want me to leave. Of course not. She had been such a lonely child that it was easy for me to start playing a large role in her life. Too easy. I worried about it, it would be unforgivable if I had achieved nothing except "stirring her up" as I had put it once, words which had made her so indignant. I found myself thinking of her as a reason even for remarrying in order to make her a happier childhood. I imagined visiting Chagrin Falls with her. Rediscovering Jean's past with her. Then again I felt all that was selfish and sentimental nonsense.

She brought me her school workbooks with her sums and stories and she wanted me to give her "examinations." As far as I can judge such things, she was bright, but she needed constant reassurance and if I found fault with her about anything, the light in her face would vanish as if switched off.

One Saturday she showed me a lesson they had had at school on "the atom." It had been a week of antinuke demonstrations in the south of France, and the teacher had told the children that nuclear power was a great and beneficial invention like electricity and pasteurization. All I said to that was that her mother would not agree, and without another word Beatrix tore out the pages and crumpled them up in the ashtray. She then wanted me to set fire to them and burn them but I convinced her the tearoom would not appreciate that.

She had lent me her picture of Jean, and Monsieur Toch the photographer made two large prints from it, one for her, one for me. She had not known that could be done and was ecstatic about it. I said, it was a bit by way of a farewell present, I'd have to go soon, but I would see to it we would get together again.

She asked, "Where do you have to go back to?"

"Well, to nowhere really."

"Do you have a new ladyfriend in America?"

"No, Jeanie."

"Then why?"

"I'm in limbo here."

She stared at me and I went on, "You don't know what that is, it's hard to explain. I am—"

"I know what limbo is," she interrupted. "It is hard to explain that you are an unbaptized baby, David." At that, she began to laugh which was a great relief, to both of us. I said she was a wise girl, and not to worry. All would end well.

When I got back to the hotel I was received very gravely; the receptionist and the proprietress told me in chorus, "A convocation, for you," and watched how I would cope with the shock.

It was a summons to report to the Commissariat of the 7th Arrondissement in Rue Amélie, and when I just stuffed it in my pocket, the proprietress literally paled with disapproval. Later that evening she asked me how much longer I was staying.

"Not much longer," I assured her.

56.

"YOU'VE GIVEN UP THEN," the major said when I told him I'd be going home soon. No, I had not; there was nothing to give up on or persevere with.

He said he was sorry to see me go. "Actually I was told to phase out your job immediately," he told me with a little grin. "'Phase out immediately.' Even the language has been turned into soya paste. You leave when you are good and ready." He then invited me to dinner at his house for the following evening.

I showed up on his doorstep (of an impressively posh pavilion in a courtyard on Rue de Vaugirard), clutching a bunch of roses, tiny ones but two francs apiece. Ten roses: one half the body of the purple-haired girl. I had not even known if there existed a Mrs. Pitman, but indeed there was, thin and aristocratic-looking and quite a bit younger than he.

The major was in a red dinner jacket, resplendent, and we sat down to dinner at a long, narrow table of polished wood, on high-backed chairs as in a church pew. The food was served by a disgruntled-looking Frenchwoman, the sister of the concierge, as the major's wife told me with a sad little smile—sad, presumably, at the thought of a more elegant past.

Those two, the major and his wife, conversed: not chit-chat along "And where are you from?" lines, but discussion of general subjects. At one point the major explained the beauty of natural logarithms to us. They had a sense of humor, though, and the more they provided me with openings to say something clever or amusing too, the less I rose to the occasion and the more boring and clumsy I appeared to myself.

They were archconservative but not the know-nothing conservatism you get from the bar patrons in Rockville Centre. They passed at a fast clip from Cubans to Swedes, admired the West Germans, pitied idealists. They had no illusions about human nature which would never change but would have been the first to cheer if we had been created otherwise. I raised some objection because I felt I had to, and Mrs. Pitman answered in a way to make me seem less heavy-handed than I was.

"Do you ride?" she asked me, and when I said no, she told me I was bound to be good with horses, she could tell from my hands.

I looked down on those hands, one holding a coffee cup, one lying on the almost black wood of the dining table: they are small for a man, and narrow, with long fingers. This riding angle was new, but I had been told by women that I would surely be a fine pianist (I cannot even carry a tune). How easy it is, I thought, to enter this world of theirs, to speak the language of the majoress. What a temptation really. In the lobby, on the table where she had deposited my ten roses, I had seen a portrait of a tall and thin young woman, spinstery, who resembled her, who was doubtlessly her daughter by our major or by a previous sire. I could be asked back for tea, take riding lessons in the Bois, meet the daughter—or someone's daughter—I could be her son-in-law next. All because my hands are thin and I have read a lot of books. No money? They surely wouldn't worry too much, they must both have any number of relations in the States ready to give me the proper job. A life without further shocks. Quiet good-neighborly years, enjoying your privileges, no unasked-for guilt toward the victims on this earth. Husband and father, until the final Blue Cross–Blue Shield denouement.

The major took me to his study after his wife had wished me good night and excused herself, and poured brandies. Its walls and tables were covered with the mementos and testimonials of every human battle, with tanks, cannon, and lead soldiers, World War I maps of artillery barrages marked hour by hour and stamped "Top Secret" in red, pictures of generals on horseback pointing the way forward (or backward) with their swords.

"When I was in high school," I said after my first sip, "we used to sing a song, 'Ain't gonna study war no more—'."

"You know," the major answered after a moment, "this is actually a cheap brandy, what they call a coachman's brandy. I like it better. The Grandes Fines Champagnes are too perfumed for me."

Ignoring that remark of mine was his concept of politeness, I was sure. "Yes, this is nice," I said, "I like it better too."

57.

O N A B E N C H in the Vaugirard subway station. The wind from the tunnel carried the candy wrappers on the platform back and forth. Not a soul was in sight but on the steps down an Algerian with a broom had assured me the last train was still due.

Major, madam majoress, the universe may very well have been created for no other reason than to have an earth with people on it. It is possible.

In chemistry it was pointed out to us, you will know this already, sir, that if water were not the only substance *not* to shrink all the way to its freezing point but to expand again when it gets below four centigrade, then, then what? then ice would not float but sink to the bottom of the seas, accumulate, make life impossible. The vastness around us? It gives the space and the balance for the earth's travels—I mean, life depends on a million precise conditions all coming together.

In other words, we could be right back in the center of things, back to before Copernicus. Not innocently this time but wisely. Wised up.

Imagine us in the center with circling around us the monstrous weight of dead giant planets, beyond those the infinity of glowing but equally dead stars! Alone, destroying our own world. All thinking and all sadness concentrated on this pinhead and at the mercy of men with no concept of time, chatting about History and God, ready to burn us up for the urgencies of the moment. I am garrulous, garrulously drunk on those coachman's brandies, but I see things so clearly!

But are there no causes then, nothing to die for and to kill for? Major, you are out of order with that question, pathetically so. What if there is no peace and no justice until we have make the earth a Jupiter or Uranus, a dark and silent machine?

I thought of that morning in the downpour on the shore of Oyster Bay. "Under ill-omened clouds." The consolations of that morning had gone.

There is the Little World, of love, food, war. And the real

world of endlessness, nothingness, unbearable to consider for long. Have the major and the majoress ever even looked into that world? Are they braver than I am or just more stupid?

But life is intolerable. Except for children. All we can do by way of duty is to shield our children.

Soldierliness, major, is surely on par with dogs and cats fighting. No, that is not right. In the Little World, it has great romantic possibilities and virtues. In the real world, it has no meaning.

Over the third round of brandies, the major had told a story about a British member of Parliament called Shinwell. "This Shinwell was a Jew," the major had said, "like me, and during a parliamentary debate some country squire on the opposite side of the question said to him, 'Why don't you go back to Poland.' And Shinwell stood up, walked across the floor of parliament, and slapped this man's face."

"Good."

"That is not the end of the story. A year or so ago that man who got slapped died. I read his obituary notice in the Paris *Herald Tribune*. And you know what? That was the only thing they had to say about his life, that slap he had received from Shinwell. What do you think of that, Lum?"

I had answered that it seemed terribly sad. A wasted life.

The major had lost his enthusiasm at this reply. "Yes," he had muttered. "A wasted life." And he did not make the point he had set out to make.

The subway came.

"Having seen the Pacific—" Some writer had put those words down as his salvation. A long time ago.

Having seen the Pacific. What would there be to see, now? There are no white places on the map any more, the sources of the Nile have been on television. As has the dark side of the moon. Death is the only white place left. Different from Stanley and Livingstone, we are very scared.

58.

I BADE THE MAJOR good-bye on the telephone with my regards to his wife. No teas, no riding lessons, no daughter. A last, cheerful hour with Beatrix; we wrote envelopes and put stamps on them (to David Lum, c/o Hotel Royalton) for her use, and I gave her a bunch of signed withdrawal slips for the joint savings account. She would make plans for what she would do with the money when she was older. I kissed her and we said, till soon, till very, very soon.

I packed, everything into one suitcase. I still had most of the extra week's salary the major had given me. My return ticket I had bought the day I arrived. At the hotel desk they wanted more than money, though: another summons from the Commissariat had arrived, and surely I was not just going to leave? No, no, I'd go by on my way to the airport. Studying the thing, I discovered in its left-hand corner a scribble indicating a copy had been sent to "M. Alfred Garrison." Who else; it must have been the local equivalent of some kind of desist & stay-away from his daughter proceedings. I threw it away, and then I boarded the bus out to the Paris airport for the noon plane.

But once I had arrived there and stood in the light rain in front of the terminal building with my bag, I turned around and went back into town.

It was a quite rational knowledge/fear that I had missed

out, left out I don't know what. I knew I would be a lost soul if in eight hours I would be standing on the sidewalk at Kennedy among the Carey Bus men and the *New York Posts*. I needed time. I was also coping with a premonition that if I went back I would make some mad or deadly move after one night alone in the Royalton, really alone this time. The other possibility, that I would try to forget the whole business, go back to normal and to a new job, a new little apartment, complete with a deepfreeze and space for a new Mrs. Lum, did not seem any better.

Back on the Paris streets, I felt precisely as I did when I was a kid standing on the high diving board for the first time: a feeling in the pit of my stomach that I was going to do something I did not want to do. I walked into a department store and bought a white shirt, and outside in the street I bought a bow tie from a peddler's cart. Then I took the subway to the Austerlitz station from which the trains for Blois in the Loire valley leave, something I knew from when I had toyed with this same plan earlier in my stay. The estate of Garrison's mother was near Blois.

Trying on the shirt in the department store, I had seen I still had the major's library card in my pocket; in the station I took three pictures of myself in a machine and I stapled one of them over his, at the counter of a Xerox shop. It looked all right. I telephoned Garrison to make sure he was in Paris; he answered the telephone and I said, wrong number. Then I got on the next train to Blois.

I had not realized it was a train ride of three hours. I arrived in the dark; it was eight o'clock. I checked into a hotel across the station and was about to telephone Mrs. Garrison and make an appointment for the next day, but hung up at the last moment. She might call her son. It was better just to show up at a workaday time like nine in the morning. I learned that her place, called Château de Molineuf, was ten kilometers away and that I would need a taxi and keep it waiting. That would help make an impression, though.

It was a nice ride early in the day, right through the woods, "Blois Forest," the cab driver informed me. The "château" was less grand than I had expected but it was a mansion all right. I announced myself to the maid as Captain Jack Pitman, for that was what it said on the library card. I waved it but neither she nor Mrs. Garrison, who received me immediately, looked at it. When I told Mrs. Garrison I was completing a file on the former Mrs. Alfred Garrison III, née Jean More, she was about to have me turned out, but when I hastily added no one would ever bother her after this, the More woman was under arrest and this was to dispose of the case once and for all, she looked happy again and ready for a nice chat. "I'm glad to hear that," she said, "glad simply as a citizen. My poor son. He thought I was old-fashioned. Too circumspect. He was disabused soon enough."

It was strange sitting there. My first imitation of Jean's underground way of doing things. It had a taste of crime even, this Captain Pitman business, but it came surprisingly easy. Once I heard myself talking I felt fine. Mrs. Garrison asked me if I had spoken to her son yet and I answered that it would be less painful to him if I covered the personal aspects with her first. "We don't like to bother our colleagues in the Foreign Service more than necessary," I said. I had spent an hour on my appearance and my button-down shirt was as neat as only brand-new shirts are.

59.

JEAN MORE HAD COME to Europe after graduation and met Alfred Garrison at a Fourth of July reception in the Paris embassy, or at least that was Mrs. Garrison's understanding.

"It wouldn't have been at the reception for the general public," she assured me, "Alfred always stays away from those. Miss More may have crashed the party he attended or then again I seem to recall her father being a state senator or having some such métier—that kind of people travel with letters of introduction—with just enough substance to them that you cannot totally ignore them—"

Six weeks later they got married, while she was away in Biarritz. She had tried everything to discourage the relationship, "everything within reason," one could not order a Garrison and secretary of embassy about. Alfred had had no experience with women, although he was terribly attractive. "He still is, Captain, as you will see." But he was reticent, and then, she had set him high standards, which nowadays—

She had written an old friend in Washington to learn more about the girl. In typical Washington manner, when he finally answered the couple had already been back from their honeymoon for two months and the girl was already "as we say in France, 'in an interesting condition'—in this case, 'infuriating' would have been a better word than interesting! And imagine the shock! She was wanted by the FBI! 'Inciting to riot.'" Alfred had turned chalk white when she showed him the letter.

Mrs. Garrison had wanted to aim for an annulment and to get the ambassador behind a fast extradition but Alfred had refused the embarrassment. He had not said one word about it to the More girl, not for seven months, and then when she came home from her lying-in he had the papers ready, she signed everything, she had no choice, had she, and Alfred took custody of the baby and the girl was on a plane back to Oklahoma or wherever she was from. But he had not notified the American police, as part of the agreement.

"I still think my first reaction was sounder, the child has been no credit to the Garrison name," Mrs. G. said. "And there you have the whole story. Technically, I have often thought, we were guilty too, of harboring a fugitive. I hope you are not going to arrest me, Captain."

We both smiled at the idea.

"Where did they go on their honeymoon?" I asked.

For the first time she really looked at me, and with sudden suspicion. "Why would anyone want to know that, ten years later?"

"We don't," I said quickly. "Idle curiosity."

"Oh—to Greece, Skyros. Alfred had rented a villa on the island from a friend at the Athens embassy. A friend of my late husband's. Without asking me. My husband and I once spent an Easter there, long ago. A comfortable house. Full of Victoriana. Right on the beach. No tourists, you know. Not then, anyway. The natives use the beach for a road only."

Back on the train, looking out over the bare fields gliding by.

A house on a beach, full of Victoriana. Jean wakened by the whirring and rattling of a grandfather clock just before it strikes. She slipped out of bed without looking at the curled up figure of Alfred next to her and tiptoed down the stairs. Moonlight shone in through French windows. She slowly walked around the room and for the first time, in the peculiar black-white illumination of a moonlit night, she studied all those objects d'art and bric-a-brac which Alfred's father's friend from Athens had collected.

How ugly they must have appeared or worse than ugly, false. She resisted the impulse to break off a shepherd's head with its curls and pink grin. That would not do at all, this was Dresden, "fetching very high prices at Sotheby's these days." She studied the clock, silent now but for its merciless tick. On its face, sun, moon, and stars were depicted, all as little men with big heads. Beside it, a glass cabinet with wax seals and Tanagra figures. Why knock it, if it makes them happy. But how draining it would be to live a lifetime with things of such desperate joylessness.

She had opened the French windows and walked down a path and out onto the beach, careful where she put her bare feet. A soft Mediterranean night. She started walking close to the sea which broke soundlessly on the sand. From far off she saw a black mass move toward her and it frightened her for a moment until it dissolved, into two mules with people walking behind them. The mules were loaded with sacks, the people turned out to be two old or old-looking women carrying sticks to keep the beasts going.

Then she was all alone. There was a line of color in front of her over the eastern sea, the wine-colored sea which touches Asia at its other shore. She felt a turbulence in her of conflicting emotions and impulses, she pulled her nightgown off over her head and draped it on a rock. She stood in the sand, naked, then she went to wet her hands in the sea and touched her body. It made her shiver with cold and she could smell the salt. Perhaps in that second she knew already that her years of thinking about life had been no help at all, that she had been nothing but a schoolgirl just turned eighteen who had been on a temporary high, created by ambassadors and being waited on by French butlers and the breathlessness of parties where jazz quartets played in Louis Seize settings. A world which for one long beat would have seemed on a higher level of awareness and happiness than that of peace meetings on a dirty street of downtown Chicago or the stillness of Chagrin Falls, shattered only by chain saws and the radio from an open convertible full of kids going by.

I was certain that she had not loved Alfred Garrison and that she had not liked him then and that he did not like her. He kept his eyes closed when he made love to her, and his face turned red, he was aggressive. He assumed she'd hate it, he was using her and not even for his pleasure but to perpetuate himself.

There you are, she had thought, standing naked at the edge of the sea, that's how the ball bounces as we used to say. Perhaps his mother will start liking me, perhaps I'll stay with her a lot, in the country, and he and I will see each other on weekends. Perhaps I can study economics, a work-family relationship.

But then she had huddled in the sand, leaning against the rock with the nightgown on it; the stone felt warm. This once, she felt sorry for herself. She burst into tears.

60.

AT FOUR in the afternoon I was back in Paris with the pleasant feeling that I had achieved something: not my learning about that marriage, which I had all pretty well guessed, but my getting away from perpetual normalcy by being Captain Pitman. Not always being an onlooker.

Then, standing motionless on the platform of the Austerlitz railroad station with the passengers pushing past me on
each side, I sank back into gloom. What now?

I checked my suitcase and studied the wall map at the
entrance to the subway. Beatrix, the major, a hotel—I
could think of nothing I wanted except for going to the
library (which would close at six), and seeing the purple-
haired girl. I had a hundred and fifty francs left. First I
bought a writing pad. Making a list or a schedule always
helps me when I'm in a muddle.

She was at her post in the Rue Saint-Denis doorway talking with another girl. I did not immediately notice her, for
her hair had now become orange-blond, sedate by com-
parison. I was taken aback by that moment of nonrecog-
nition, enough to start out this time by asking her name. I
did not want her to evaporate namelessly from my life.
Elaine. Elaine, and she also volunteered that she lived in
Ville D'Avray; both girls determinedly repeated that name
till I had it. She came in by train to the job. "Do you have
a commuters ticket?" I asked, and they laughed at that. I
must add that I already knew it is next to impossible for a
foreigner to say something which will be considered amusing by a Frenchman, let alone by a French woman or rather
girl with a Star Trek face. On the strength of it, those two
accepted my invitation to go have a drink together.

There I was, one moment a lost and pale foreigner, the
next moment sitting in a bar like a Marseilles pimp, or the
way I see a Marseilles pimp, with two girls sipping green
liqueurs and talking to each other in low voices, taking my
presence for granted. I could see from my reflection in the
bar mirror that I looked different already, tougher, cool,
without that hangdog expression.

Both girls had digital watches, new ones, for they made a
ceremony out of checking the time on them. I tried to have
them stay put by suggesting another round. I liked this new

Marseilles style, I could not bear the thought that it would not have lasted more than twenty-five minutes by the bar clock.

But they had to get going. "Do you want it, now?" my Elaine asked. Feverish sums. Those drinks—at least forty francs. Forty and forty. If I said yes, I would be back out alone on the sidewalk, a sloppy tourist once more, before it was even six o'clock, with a whole long evening to wade through.

The barman came. Eighteen francs only—that comes from not being a tourist, an outsider; everyone treats you differently.

"Give my friend a little present," Elaine told me as I was putting my change away. Outside, after the other girl had kissed her good-bye and shaken my hand, Elaine started walking me to the room, although I had not answered her question yet.

I hesitated.

"Well—?" she asked.

I said I had an appointment first and could we meet at nine? In the same bar?

"Well, yes," she answered listlessly. "Nine more or less, of course."

We shook hands but as I turned away, a man came up and accosted her. He was perfectly all right as a customer, I mean he was clean, shirt and tie, briefcase, a neat businessman between office and home, that wasn't it; for some other reason it was intolerable that this fellow was going to have her right then. I came back up to them and ignoring him, said to her, "Wait. No. I'm staying."

"Et alors," from the briefcase man.

Elaine looked furiously at me. "And your appointment?" she asked.

"Never mind," I said, "Never mind. Here." And I gave her a hundred-franc note.

She shrugged apologetically to the businessman and climbed up the stairs ahead of me.

While she sat on the edge of the bed to take off her jeans, she said very annoyedly, "You could have waited ten minutes, no?"

She sounded so unappealing, I thought, God, what a fool I am, why did I do that? Now I'm broke. I answered, "No, I couldn't wait. You are very beautiful with your new hair."

That pleased her. For the first time she took all her clothes off, not for me, but to study herself in the mirror.

"It's not bad, is it. When I get wrinkles, I'll kill myself. With sleeping pills," she said matter of factly.

Wrinkles is *rides,* a word I did not know or recognize, and from the rest of the sentence I thought it meant some awful disease.

"What?" I asked. "What's that?"

"Wrinkles! Like you have!" And she pulled her face down to show me.

I was indeed back out on the sidewalk before six, as a pale, near-penniless outsider. I had told Elaine to be in the bar at nine all the same, but that was bluff, I had neither the money left nor the desire.

The hundred-franc turn had not been very nice. Maybe it was better when she just stripped her jeans down. I went into a café toilet and washed as much of myself as I could manage, and dried myself off with my handkerchief. I started walking. I came to a side street which looked shabbier than Rue Saint-Denis and took it.

An eat shop had Arabic script only on the window plus a big "Twelve Francs" painted in yellow. I went in and pointed at the "Twelve" sign and they brought me a plate and a terrine with a kind of gooey rice in meat sauce. You are not supposed to eat it all when they do that, but I did and when the waiter came to take the terrine away and saw it was empty, he angrily pointed me out to the man who was doing the cooking. I put twelve francs on the table and got out of there, back to the bar where I had been with the girls. I had four francs left but never mind, I ordered a Scotch. That same barman now did not even seem to recognize me. It was still only seven o'clock.

I drank a lot of whiskey which helped, and got into discussions with several people. One of them was an American who told me our politicians would have us all killed. I nodded, but he got furious all the same, repeating, "But I mean it! I mean it literally!" When Elaine came back in there, it was half past nine and I was no longer drunk, just sick to my stomach. She accepted the offer of a drink but kept standing at the bar with it. She did not want to sit at my table, she bent over and asked, "You want to, again?" and when I shook my head, she said, "Till tomorrow then." We shook hands. It was nice to be on a handshake basis.

I could not work up the courage to tell the barman I had no money. That is another of those actions which do not fit into normalcy, like presenting yourself under a false name. I have made the you-wash, I-dry joke a hundred times, and spending a night in a police station would not matter either, so who cares? But the reality of this barman looked more as if he would knock my teeth out. Still, it was not even fear of that. It was the hesitancy to abandon the comfort of being one of the crowd, to abandon being accepted, doing what you are expected to do. That is as near as I can describe it.

The problem was solved abjectly by me. I went to the counter and muttered that I had lost my wallet, and while the barman hovered over me, I telephoned, heaven help me, to the major. I ruined the major for evermore; that is to say, I could never face him again after that. I put the barman on and the major said he was an American diplomat and knew me, and spelled out his address and would stand guarantee for my drinks, after which I slinked out of there.

I returned to my New Year's Eve park and lay down on the bench (the canvas chair had disappeared) and dozed off. I woke when it started to rain; I stood it for a long time, taking pleasure in this chastisement. But then I caved in on that score, too, and walked all the way back to my old hotel. The night man was up and about and after checking that my old room was free, he put me in there. I spread my wet clothes out over the radiator, huddled under the covers and pulled them up over my head.

When I was warm, I stuck my head back out and lay looking at the gray oblong of the window. It was a very dark night. I could not sleep, I did not want to sleep.

I felt guilty, without understanding of what.

61.

WHEN I WAS A CHILD, an aunt or great-aunt visited us at Christmas time in Connecticut. She was an old woman and she told me that her grandmother had seen the Emperor Napoleon when he paid a state visit to Leewarden, the town in Holland where her branch of the family was from. She even remembered an anecdote about the trouble the schoolchildren of that town had had with learning to cry *"Vive l'Empereur!"*

I had known a woman who had known a woman who laid eyes on Napoleon.

Time is easily bridged and moves fast. And all experience of mankind fits into one very large cooking pot.

Too much fuss is made, maybe.

I had been to the Arc de Triomphe, sitting within a square called Etoile which is star, where they have a gas flame burning for the Unknown Soldier. I fell in with a tour guide telling his group that the arch was so many meters high and so many wide and so on. A German with short gray hair and a magnificent camera hanging from his neck said that Albert Speer, a German architect, had already had a similar monument designed and ready for Hitler, except that it was to be ten times as big. That got a mixed bag of smiles from everyone. The man with the camera did not look to me as if he had meant it as a joke, though. Perhaps he felt that after the next war it would still be built. And why not. I've had ladies at New York cocktail parties tell me that we should have let Hitler finish the job in Europe first: killing off the Russians, they meant. My visit to the Arc de Triomphe was when I worked for the major and had some money in my pocket. It must have been a Saturday or Sunday when I was wandering all over town.

The thought of Suleiman Alepin has come back to me erratically ever since I read about him in the Bibliothèque Nationale. He was that young man who killed General Kléber in Cairo. I have wondered if Cairo has an Alepin Street. Kléber has one of the nicest and widest avenues of Paris, with a double row of trees and so many double- and triple-parked cars that they look as if they had been abandoned by a fleeing population, as in that futuristic movie with Charlton Heston the last survivor in New York or Los Angeles. The French triumphal arch sits in a star of avenues and Avenue Kléber is one of them.

Alepin's deed is not beyond my comprehension. Indeed not. I have repeated it. I have stepped into the shady palace gardens from a dusty Cairo square and have felt the relief of thus ending a day of feverish thoughts of martyrdom, thoughts I had toyed with the way you toy with a sore tooth.

I stood in the path of the general and looked in his pale

face with the streaks of sweat running from under his hat into his preposterously heavy woollen collar, looked at his stomach bulging under the white and gold waistcoat, saw him not-see me, dark little native, and easily forgetting his being a man I stabbed my dagger into that uncomfortable flesh.

But after that it became obscure. I could conjure up thoughts of a daring escape or a speech about liberty in front of my judges. These remained thoughts. I could not see this.

I could not see myself stand (or do they make you sit?) while they pushed my hand into a fire.

The idea that but for a different turn of fate I could have been born to feel a stake enter my bowels was not only nauseating, it was not really understandable.

But since I could have done the deed, have done the deed, why should I not understand what Alepin had no choice but to understand? By what dispensation was Alepin's fate and way of dying beyond my comprehension?

The gray oblong of the window in my room began to lighten. I got up and put my clothes on. It was so early when I came down to the hotel desk that the night man was still on duty. I asked him if he could cash a check for me. He said yes, but then it turned out he meant a Traveler's Check. "Oh damn," I said, "I know I can cash a Traveler's Check. A personal check." I had written one for fifty dollars on the Merchant Bank of Hempstead, L.I. He vanished with it and reappeared with the lady of the hotel in her dressing gown who held it between thumb and forefinger. "It is in dollars," she said, registering the utmost in human astonishment. "We cannot, obviously—"

"Never mind, never mind!"

She took a deep breath. "Last night, at six in the evening, a policeman came by. It appears you still have not answered your summons. I must insist—"

"I'm going there right now," I cried, snatching the check out of her hand. She did not try to stop me when I went through the door; she did not know my suitcase was not in my room but at the station.

62.

I STARTED WALKING. I was unshaven and my clothes were stiff from having dried on the radiator but I was all right. I came to the point called Etoile again, and wandered up and down each of the avenues of that star. They were eleven or twelve in all, I lost count. It was an exhausting ritual.

I went to sit on a café terrace on Avenue Kléber and saw the Arc de Triomphe, sideways, bare trees framing a stone rectangle lit by the sun. A triumph. The blue Etoile name signs had "General de Gaulle" tacked onto them but no one whom you ask the way calls it that. Caesar rode through the city with his enemies in chains dragged along behind him, Eisenhower the same up Broadway with ticker tape and minus enemies in chains. De Gaulle walked up here with German snipers still firing. Kléber never got home of course. Napoleon was probably too sophisticated for that kind of stuff, but he must have felt as good as any of them on March 20, 1815, when he had come back from Elba and rode into Paris in the evening, in a pouring rain, and everyone was out in the street to cheer and they virtually carried him back into his own palace and tucked him into his own bed, still warm from that Louis the Seventeenth or the Eighteenth who had just made his getaway.

His night must have been undisturbed by the ghosts of a million dead privates—generals aren't that way.

The door and the windows of the café were closed and steamed over and no one but me was on the terrace, it was much too cold. After a while a waiter came out all the same, and I got up and walked on.

I thought, doesn't New York have some kind of tree, the name escapes me, the only species that survives the fumes and the carbon monoxide and the excretions of a million dogs? These trees don't look like it at all, and won't the trees of Paris soon be dead then? Perhaps along this star of avenues the people of Paris will put up aluminum trees with green nylon leaves, very pretty, they could use them for parking, hoisting up one car into each tree, vertically.

I bought a loaf of bread and ate as I pursued my way back toward the river. I descended the steps to the quay and came to the vault of a bridge, and here the cobblestones had been covered with old sacks filled with what felt like newspaper. I made up a corner against the curved stone and sat down with the remainder of my bread.

It was silent there, the noise of the cars going by overhead was muffled as through a stone wall. Thus a prisoner in an old fortress must hear what is going on outside his walls. A feeling of security, too.

Darkness fell.

The river to the left of me was black and without any lights; to the right I could see only a column of the bridge which cut off the view. I chewed on my bread and had a kind of peace come over me, I imagined I was getting near understanding. Then shuffled steps became audible and I tried to block them out, an interruption would be terrible. It was no use, though. Someone shook my arm.

I smelled and I saw an old man, who spoke a long sentence I did not understand.

"My place," he then said, pointing at the sacks.

"Go to hell," I said in English.

He did not protest, he stood still and stared at me.

With a sigh I moved away and sat down on the stones at the other end of the vault, and he began rearranging everything the way it had been before. But then he took two of the sacks and brought them over to me. I nodded and accepted them; those stones were hard and cold and wet. After that, the man kept staring at me, but I looked away. I looked out over the almost invisible black surface of the water and tried to get back to that clear moment. It came back. The old man sharing his bedding for the night was not an interruption, to the contrary.

I understand, perhaps.

63.

THEY DO make you sit down. My feet are shackled, they make me sit down on a stool. A masked hangman, half-naked, presses down on my shoulders, another grabs my right arm and pushes my hand into the flame. The shock is so violent that for one instant I succeed in pulling back, although the man is a giant, and we tug with my hand in and out of the fire. Then my resistance is gone and he holds it there.

It is done. I am lying on the ground. Urine is running down my legs and the two men are grinning, I cannot see the grins under their black masks but I hear the laughter in their throats.

They tear off my clothes. I think there are three now, I am not certain, and they drag me outside, it must be outside, I feel the heat of the sun. A roar of voices, staring eyes. They take the shackles off my feet and for a second I do not understand why. A wooden stake sticks out of the ground, and they hold me above it with my legs spread wide. I am held upright with my arms pinned behind my back and I am pushed down upon that stake in one violent shove. They still hold my arms, and one of those men starts pulling down on my feet.

I feel no pain, none at all.

The mystery of Alepin's fate is that the same is in store for me after all. I will die as slowly. Blinded, my skin burned off, a casualty of future war. The atomic war will even all accounts.

All guilt will be exonerated.

I slept.

Later in the night my neighbor offered me a swig from his bottle of wine. I thought the alcohol would take care of the germs and drank.

When day broke, I got up, added my two sacks to the sleeping old man's cover, and climbed up to the street. I managed to find a city bus going in the direction of the airport, and another bus after that. It took hours but I had no money left for the real airport bus.

At the TWA departure counter they did not receive me very enthusiastically. I looked repulsive. I had my ticket, though, and after they had made me go through the security gate twice and held my passport up to the light, I got on the noon plane. Only when I was standing in the Kennedy customs line did I think of my suitcase in the locker of the Austerlitz railroad station.

64.

I WAS LUCKY. New York was having one of those spells of amazing weather it comes up with at times and it was already like spring. Things looked friendlier. My room in the Royalton was as I had left it, and at the unemployment office on Sixth Avenue they accepted my statement that I had been ill and they paid me for two weeks. If it had been snowing, they would have refused.

I sat in my room writing job applications; I had copied lists of possible openings from the commercial aviation directories at the Public Library. It was evening. After two hours with that, I decided to write a letter to Beatrix in Paris. I did the envelope, "Miss Beatrix Garrison, 9, Boulevard Suchet, Paris 16, France," and stopped. It looked odd, an address too remote, too unrelated to my rooftop view of West 44th Street. I put a sheet of paper in front of me and wrote, "Dearest Jean," and stared at the Royalton wallpaper, royal lilies actually, a design straight from the bedchamber of Louis the Fourteenth. There was nothing to say. I drew some five-pointed stars, my favorite doodle, and went to bed.

It was still dark when my telephone rang. I turned on the light, six o'clock on my watch. The telephone could not be reached from the bed. I jumped out and picked it up. It was Beatrix, in a voice which was a mixture of excitement and defiance.

I sat down at my table, looking at that sheet of paper which had failed to become a letter to her, and said, "Hello Beatrix. Hello Jean. How nice to hear your voice!"

"Are you sure it's nice?"

"It is wonderful. But you know, it's only six in the morning here."

There was a little laugh at the other end. "And how is the weather?" she asked.

"God, I don't know. I haven't looked yet. I'm cold sitting here."

"I'll tell you," she said. "It's going to be a nice day. And I'm at the airfield. At Kennedy airfield. At the Air France counter."

I told her to stay put right there and wait for me. "Don't budge. Ne bougez pas. Don't let anyone take you any-where." Fortunately I had already fetched my car back from Newark. I jumped into my clothes and drove out there as fast as I could. On the way I did not even try to figure out what to do, I just played the radio.

I shouted, "One minute, this is an emergency!" at the cops in front of the terminal and ran in. In spite of that voice of hers on the telephone I had thought to find a bedraggled child, a stowaway perhaps with a security man, tapping his foot, beside her. But Beatrix was not to be un-derestimated. She was sitting behind the Air France coun-ter in a green wintercoat and a fur hat, with very elegant pieces of luggage at her feet. I felt different and happy the moment I saw her.

"There's my uncle," she said. "Thank you so much!" And she shook hands with an Air France lady, ducked across to the other side, and kissed me.

"Thank you," I repeated lamely to the lady. "Sorry I was late."

And I followed Beatrix with her luggage out of the building.

I opened my car door for her but she said, "Wait. This comes first." She took a letter out of her purse and put it in the mailbox at the entrance.

"All right, Uncle," she said.

"What was that?"

"I wrote it on the plane. It's to my daddy."

"Saying what?"

"That I have gone back to my mother. He's away. He'll find it when he comes back to Paris. He's with *his* mother, so 'fair is fair,' I wrote."

65.

PRESUMABLY I WAS DOING the wrong thing but I never worried about it from the moment we drove off. We were going on a pilgrimage, or to be more low-keyed, on a reconnaissance. It was that, low-keyed. We set out to trace Jean's steps as far back as we could; we were rebuilding half of Beatrix's childhood for her, the half she had been cheated of. We were very matter-of-fact about it. Not sentimental. Happy.

Before I was even out of Kennedy, Beatrix had convinced me that she was not the least tired and did not wish to be put in bed. And without deliberating on it, I turned off the Van Wyck Expressway and drove out onto the Island and to Rockville Centre. "We'll begin where Jean and I lived last," I said. "It isn't much of a place, but we were very happy there, she was, too."

My heart was beating in my throat as I drove up that familiar street to the garage apartment. The traffic was thick and I had to go past once and around the block before I could stop near the door.

"Well, there it is."

"Where? It's boarded up, David."

So it was. I had been afraid to look properly; the windows upstairs and downstairs had metal sheets over them but the garage door was half-raised.

We double-parked and went in. A man stood there, busy pulling on a pair of overalls over his clothes. "Can I help you folks?" he asked.

"Just looking," I said. "I used to live here."

"It's been sold. It's going to be a takeout franchise."

"Can we go upstairs?"

"Fine with me. Watch your step on the stairs."

It was half-dark in our apartment, with only the light from the doorway and along the edges of the boarding. The place was bare. When my eyes had become adjusted, I could see the outline on the wall where the refrigerator had been. We could smell the chalky dust rising from below where the man had started banging away. Bits of linoleum were still stuck to the floor planks.

"Don't drive yet," Beatrix asked when we were back in the car, and she rolled down the window and gave the building a long look. "That's one," she said.

"Well, I'm sorry, they sure act fast here. There was some nice stuff in there. A good bed."

"Yours?"

"Yes. It's just as well though. Shall we go now?"

"Yes."

Out of the corner of my eye I saw her wave at the place. I had thought of going to the flying school from there and that would have been a terrible mistake; how could I have planned such a thing? If at all, that is where we must go last. Perhaps then it will make sense to her. And to me.

"We're going to Chagrin Falls," I said. "To your mommy's old school."

"Today?"

"Why not? It'll be a two-day drive, I think."

For I had decided that I should check out of the Royalton straightaway if I did not want us to be caught by Garrison.

"Look," Beatrix said, and she waved a handful of money in front of my face. "A thousand dollars."

"How did you get that?"

"Harriet's brother helped me. She has a brother who is nearly grown up. He came to the bank with me, you know, our savings bank, yours and mine. I don't know what he said, but he made it work. Harriet's a friend of mine in school. Not a real friend. I gave her brother a hundred dollars."

"No!"

"He had asked for two hundred," she told me with a satisfied smile.

I shaved in two minutes and checked out of the hotel while she waited in the car, and by mid-morning we were driving west on Route 80 through New Jersey, Beatrix asleep on the back seat.

66.

I THOUGHT SHE WOULD be cranky when she woke up. My knowledge of children stems mostly from their behavior in TV commercials. She was not, and our lunch of hamburgers and milkshakes in a roadside place excited her very much. This was her first day in America.

Afterward, driving that long stretch through Pennsylvania, we played Twenty Questions. That got boring and we fell silent. The low sun had vanished behind a wintry haze, and it was bleak out there. In a lonely house we passed, the lights in a downstairs room went on. Two children were bicycling toward it. She looked at them for as long as she could. "We should do some school," I said. "We don't want you to get behind. Are you good at math?"

"David," she asked, "Are you cross I came? I mean, that I came without telling?"

"I'm very glad."

"Really?"

"Really really."

"Hurrah!" she said. "And I never have to go back?"

I made a face at her.

"Do I?"

"Well," I said, "you'll have to go back some time, I guess. But it won't be the same, you'll know your mother then, you'll know who you are. No one can steal that back from you. It will go fast, you'll be sixteen before you know it, and you can go to school here in the U.S. To college."

"And you'll be there?"

"Absolutely."

"Now tell me about Jean's war," she asked.

It took me some seconds to remember where she had those words from. Jean's war for children, I had told her in Paris. "Well—"

"You're not going to fob me off!" she cried.

"Fob you off? Where did you get that expression?"

"Are you going to?"

"No."

Jean's war.

"Do you believe in God?" I asked.

She said yes.

"Well, there's God, and the Devil, and the best trick of the Devil is that he gives people comfortable reasons to do evil, I mean, people always think they just have to wage one more war, one more this or that, and for the best of reasons this time, for of course they are totally different from the people in the past who had no good reasons when they did the cruel and terrible things they did."

[166]

"Like burning Jeanne d'Arc at the stake," she said.

"Precisely! If right now someone would suggest to burn a girl at the stake in the national interest, he'd be locked up as crazy, but if he suggests ten million people may have to be burned to death in the national interest, he'll be listened to. In the meantime, other people get the bombs and rockets ready to do this. They make bags of money in the process but they don't lose any sleep, they're sure it's all for the best of reasons and the guys at the other side do the same."

"I don't know what you're talking about, David," she said sternly.

Wilkes-Barre. A blue and white sign had loomed up and fallen away, saying Route 115, Wilkes-Barre. Why did it echo—that was the second landing-stop-to-be for Jean's triangle flight.

"Well, Jean-Beatrix," I said, "I know, I say 'well' too often. Your mother told me. Well, this is a greedy world and many people don't care how they make a buck. A dollar. Money. Your mother worked in a factory where they make those bombs. And she found out that they are deadly even before they are used. They poison the country. They poison children and babies, especially. Jean, your mother, declared war on them. It's not over. But we will win."

She was silent for a long time. "My mommy worked in a factory?" she then asked, her voice going up to a high *C*. "Like Algerians do?"

Miss Garrison IV. "Like many other people. That was not the point, the point—"

"The point is that she died, David."

"She fell, she fell in battle."

"Oh," she said.

I think she was afraid just then to ask more. She had turned very pale.

"You know what, we're going to sleep in a motel tonight," I said. "I bet you've never done that. And you can have anything for dinner you like."

67.

CHAGRIN FALLS high school was large and modern, low-lying behind the playgrounds which separated it from the road, Route 422, on which we came in from the metropolis, Cleveland.

Beatrix and I sat in a coffee shop on the little town square and I telephoned the dean of the school, who proved to be a lady who had been there only a short time. She put me on to her oldest administrative assistant, a Miss Fisher who remembered Jean and said, yes, she would see me. During the phone conversation she turned from amiable to reserved and I convinced Beatrix to let me go over alone first.

Miss Fisher's reserve had been caused by her still remembering an FBI visit a decade ago. When I told her I was not only no government person but had brought Jean's daughter to see the school, that Jean was dead, and that her daughter had been in America only two days and was actually waiting in my car across the road, she became very concerned and excited. I think she was that rare creature (I think it is rare), someone who had been a radical in the late sixties and still was now. I use the word "radical" loosely for want of a more precise one. A kind of enthusiastic decency, almost embarrassing in its tirelessness.

Miss F. wanted me to go and get Beatrix immediately, but I asked her to tell me the facts from Jean's past first.

And these were undramatic, pathetically so. Jean had been indicted on inciting-to-riot and other charges after a school sit-in which had led to a dozen kids in hospital, a police car overturned and burned, and looting and stone throwing in Hough, a black area of Cleveland. No, Jean had not been expelled. She and one or two teachers had spoken up for her. Jean and three other students had been given appalling terms, two years in a state correctional institution. They had appealed, there seemed a consensus then that their judge was slightly mad, and after a hearing another judge had freed them on their parents' recognizance.

The cases did not come up again until a year or more later. Jean, who had gone to Europe, had not returned and that was when the FBI was brought in. "That was of course after the car crash," Miss F. said. Did I not know about that? About Jean's parents who had been killed in a car crash in the winter of 1970, "in that terrible week when we had nothing but fog and sleet?" Jesus. I sat there, shaking my head, for Jean's parents, for the week of sleet, for the FBI who had turned a woman's life inside out because she had not been back for a second trial. Her codefendants had received suspended sentences, Miss F. told me. Jean had been cast in the role of the instigator of all that had happened there.

I went to get Beatrix. Miss F. had promised not to mention any of this with her.

I slowly walked out the long driveway and stood on the edge of Route 422, waiting for a gap in the traffic, muttering curses at the trucks rolling down the hill. It felt as bitter as if this had happened not ten years but a week ago. I put a smile on for Beatrix but she was too intrigued by it all as we drove back up to the school to pay attention to my face. She and Miss F. got on beautifully. Miss F. (she told us everyone called her that) had liked Beatrix's mother very much. She thought Beatrix looked exactly like her, and she couldn't believe Beatrix was only just ten and had never been in America before.

We entered an empty classroom where she had Beatrix sit in Jean's old place or what could have been her old place, and another classroom where she interrupted a lesson to introduce her to the teacher who said yes, he remembered Jean very well. "It's beautiful, isn't it?" Beatrix whispered to me. "We don't have all that. And they're so free." The children were seated at little tables, more or less at random, and everywhere there were drawings and plants and all sorts of exhibits. I had never been in a school which looked like that either. Then Miss F. took us to the cafeteria where I got everyone a soda, and she told Beatrix, "This is a new extension, in your mother's time it wasn't this nice. I hope you'll come to Chagrin Falls High too."

"Can I, David?" Beatrix asked.

Well—

The visit was such a success that when Miss F. heard we were traveling together but did not know yet where to stop over, she invited us to stay the night with her. She lived in a ramshackle gray-shingled house halfway down the hill toward town.

That evening I told her how Jean had been sent packing by her Paris American husband and asked if she had any idea where she could have gone to in the States. She didn't. Once Beatrix had been put to bed, Miss F.'s animation seemed to have drained away. She shook her head and I heard her mutter, "So much damage." The following morning she fed Beatrix waffles and maple syrup for breakfast. Then she had us drive her to the school and told me to wait.

She came back out five minutes later. She had Xeroxed a list for me of Jean's graduation class. Behind some names were crosses or question marks. She said, "Those are the boys and girls who were her friends."

68.

THE GRADUATION CLASS pointed us back to New York. I did not try one James Miller and an Edna Miller, for there were columns and columns of Millers in the Cleveland directory. But I got hold of the parents of a boy with a rarer name, Andrew Highsmith, through that directory. They told me Andy was in New York and gave me his telephone number. As far as they knew another boy, also marked on the graduation list, was in New York too, and he and Andy were still friends.

Back we drove, along Route 6 this time, running east along the northern border of Pennsylvania, because Route 6 was marked as "scenic" on my road map. On the way out Beatrix had said America wasn't half as pretty as all those lovely strange names of towns and rivers had led her to expect. I never asked if she liked Route 6 better. It was a change, anyway.

I had thought about just staying, about searching for a job in Cleveland and putting Beatrix in Chagrin Falls Junior High and then High. For a moment it seemed a natural thing to do, the proper sequence to our luck in coming upon someone like Miss Fisher. Then again it had no foundation except sentimentalism. "Would you really like very much to go to that school?" I had asked. "Perhaps I could find a job here."

"Perhaps," Beatrix had said. "But first we have to follow my mother's trail, don't we?"

She was more strong-willed than I, she never doubted I wanted to do that. She was aware by now that when I had described Jean to her as the avenger of wrongs during those Paris tearoom afternoons of ours, I had talked about Jean's character rather than from any intimate knowledge of Jean's life. She did not appear to resent those embroideries of mine.

The high school had been a bustling, happy place. In that green setting, with those kids in their bright clothes and their colored sneakers, so very far removed from the grime and harshness of the world, Jean could have been carefree. She could have ignored everything else and it amazed me that she had not been seduced by it. But had seeing that school helped her daughter? Maybe Jean's emergence, in all those big and little things, made her death more real and more hurtful. I wished I knew more about children. From somewhere I had stored the wisdom that they look upon a parent dying as an act of desertion, and if that were true, Beatrix could be happier for unearthing the sense in her mother's life and death.

I studied that small, determined head beside me in the car, under the short strawberry hair. I won't have children of my own, I always thought that and since my night on the wet cobblestones of the Paris embankment I was very certain of it.

I won't play that part in a future of atonement. I will be their only hostage.

This girl was as close as I would come to what I imagined that particular relationship to be.

As for Chagrin Falls, I was glad that was a reality for me now, though a less touching one than the name had been, a name which ever since Chicago used to conjure up for me a lucent picture, a waterfall, weeping willows, a young woman's melancholy—The falls are there. The counterman in the coffee shop pointed them out to Beatrix and me, "Up there, under the bridge," he said. She and I walked toward it, but then we saw a yellow excavator, sitting on that bridge, and scooping up stones and earth in a cloud of dust and grinding noise, and we turned around.

69.

ANDREW HIGHSMITH was of course no boy (in the telephone conversation with his parents we had talked about the boy Andy; I was getting confused in my generations), he was a man only ten years younger than I. He lived on the West Side, on West 82nd Street, and when I called, he said he knew no Jean More and hung up on me. We drove over and I went up to his third floor and rang the bell, with Beatrix waiting in the car. She knew now how to lock herself in.

He let me into his lobby but said again, "I don't know any Jean More. Why did you come here?"

"I was a very close friend of Jean's. I know you graduated together, and about the trial."

"I don't know what you're talking about."

I said, "Okay, just hold it a second, I'll be right back."

I ran downstairs and got Beatrix out of the car. When we were back on his floor, he stood inside but with his door open, on the chain. I saw his face change as he saw Beatrix in the uncertain light of the hallway, and he opened his door very fast. He stared at Beatrix, who stared back and then smiled at him.

"Jesus," Highsmith said.

"Her daughter."

"When she was standing outside, I figured for a moment —I thought—"

"I know."

"I'm sorry," he told me, "I thought you were another ff— another damn investigator. They used to come once a year and ask that same dumb question you asked, and once a year I answered them I knew nothing." Then he kissed

Beatrix on each cheek and hugged her. "You are the daughter of the best woman that ever was," he said.

Beatrix and I were already settled in an apartment—a small and miserable one, but an apartment, at 46 Jane Street in the Village. I had timed our getting back from Chagrin Falls to New York well, we drove into Manhattan before noon and by six I had a furnished sublet for us, three months at a hundred dollars a week. Beatrix had the bedroom and I had a cot in the other room which was really a kitchen. But we also had a bathroom with a decent shower.

I had discoursed to her about renting the place under a different name: the secret of success, I told her, was not to mess around with your own name or the name of anyone near or dear, no variations on reality, that's what got people caught—a brand-new name picked blindly was the way to do it. How? By opening a telephone book and choosing the first name in the top left-hand corner, no matter what it was.

"Okay," she said, "I'll do it for us." We had to drive around a while before we found a pay phone with a telephone directory left. Beatrix, delighted (for she loved such intrigues), opened it and looked.

"Well?" I asked.

"Hisae fish cuisine," she read off.

"Try again."

"You said the first one and never mind."

"Please try again."

She turned a block of pages and grinned.

"Well?"

"Orlando's Hair Stylist."

"Orlando—we can't be Orlando, it would sound too phoney."

"Okay. Chase Manhattan Bank," she then announced.

"Try one more time."

"Why not 'Chase'?"

So we had become Anthony Chase and daughter.

70.

J E A N   H A D   C O M E straight to New York, Andrew High-smith told us, after the Garrisons, mother and son, dispatched her from France, but it had been years before she had run into him and some other Chagrin Falls friends who had stuck together.

"The Viet war must have been just about over by then," Highsmith said, "We did not talk much about it any more, I'm sure Jean had gone on working against it, I know she was arrested during the Christmas bombing. Nothing further came of it because she called herself Beatrix Orme by then."

"In your honor," I said to Beatrix.

"She was between jobs. She had become a hotshot legal secretary who made a lot of money and she could take time out for other things. I'm a manager now by the way, for a supermarket. The one around the corner, on Amsterdam Avenue. I used to be—never mind. We had a group going, a pressure group on nuclear irresponsibility. It must have been about the time of Karen Silkwood. You know about that?"

I said I did. "I don't," Beatrix said. I told her I would explain later.

"Jean volunteered to get a job with the corporation with the worst reputation, the name is on the tip of my tongue, isn't that crazy, it's McDonald, Alson-McDonald, that's right."

"Yes. Yes."

"She mailed us her reports, for she had had to leave town, her job was somewhere in Jersey. Very incriminating things. We had two hot lawyers on our team, one of them in Washington, and they worked like crazy, to get a hearing, to get some Congressman on the stick. No soap, however."

Highsmith seemed embarrassed when he got this far.

"I've always known we let her down," he said. "We had 'No Nukes' stickers on our cars and weekly meetings in someone's living room where the wife or the girlfriend brings in sandwiches and potato chips at halftime. Jean put her whole life in it."

A silence.

"One evening," he said, "she suddenly arrived in the middle of a meeting. She said she had to make an announcement. She had got cancer and there was no doubt in her mind it was caused by the, by the Alson-McDonald industrial environment. I remember her putting it like that. No one spoke a word for about five minutes. She had a kind of smile on her face. She said, 'And I don't give a shit, if now at least you folks will get off your asses.' It was the time when the neutron bomb was first being peddled in the papers."

"Did you get off your asses?" I asked.

"We sent her to a very famous specialist, the father of a friend of a friend, a very liberal guy."

"And?"

"He said it was a radiation cancer, for sure. But he also said he couldn't be a witness to that in a court of law or in a Congressional committee."

"Because?"

Highsmith was slowing down more and more and I had to keep him going.

"Because there was no such thing as foolproof evidence

in cases of that kind, and to state otherwise would have been unscientific."

Beatrix and I looked at him and waited.

He finally finished, "After that she told us she was through with protests and petitions to Congressmen. She said she had a plan to stop the fuel rods assembly from functioning."

"How could she have done that?"

"We never knew. When she wanted to tell us about it, our lawyer said, 'We don't want to hear it, it would make us coconspirators.' We had a vote on that. The lawyer's point was carried, with only two votes against."

"What does that mean?" Beatrix asked.

"It means," I said, "that you show your hand if you agree with something. And then the people raise their hands who disagree. And then you count the hands, and who has the most wins. And only one person in there raised his hand with Jean."

"We never saw her again after the vote," Highsmith said. "And then before Christmas I read—"

"Yes, we know about that," I interrupted, in order to stop him.

Total silence. We sat around waiting no one knew for what. Beatrix got up first. "Shall we go now, David?" she asked.

Mrs. Highsmith came in just then, and everyone shook hands.

On the landing, Beatrix turned and asked, "Why did you say my mommy was the best woman ever?"

Highsmith turned red or so I thought. The light was bad. "She was brave and considerate and gentle all at the same time. We—she and I were—" He made a kind of grimace in my direction and then looked at Beatrix again. "—we had been going steady."

"And you left her," Beatrix stated.

"No, no. She left me."

His voice had become almost inaudible and I said to him, "She may have thought you'd feel sorry for her."

He shook his head. "Oh no. That wasn't it."

When we had gone down one staircase, he was still standing there.

"Andy!" Beatrix called up the stairwell. She was a surprising child all right; I did not even know she had remembered his name was Andrew.

"Andy, that only vote for her, was that your hand?"

We could just distinguish his face looking down at us.

"No, it wasn't," he said.

71.

"CANCER IS A DISEASE," Beatrix stated. Yes. Then why had I talked about Jean being a soldier and all that stuff? Because Jean had got the disease in battle, it had been no different from being wounded by a bullet. She had faced that risk voluntarily, that means, of her own will.

And that was not even how she had died, she had not died in a sick bed but in an airplane.

Beatrix was very startled at this.

No, there again it had not been blind circumstance, I assured her, she had been alone in the plane and on a mission, at action stations as they said in war.

I could not leave it at that, for Beatrix was more shaken now than when I began.

"That factory," I said, "where they are too greedy and too hasty to take care even of their own people, that place Andrew Highsmith talked about? That is where Jean got sick. And where friends of hers had miscarriages. When a baby is born dead. Jean set out to attack it."

"You mean bomb it, like in movies, like in *Flight of Eagles?*"

"Well, yes, really something like that."

"Was it a German factory?" she asked.

"It's more complicated than that. But it's something like that. An enemy factory."

"Perhaps I'll be called Beatrix again. I don't want to steal my mommy's name."

"You can share it."

In the night, I heard her cry. I waited, but then went in and sat at the foot of her bed. I stroked her hair and blew her nose for her.

"David, what happens when people die?" she asked.

"They go to heaven, most of them. Jean did."

She was quiet now, staring up at the ceiling. A little light came in from the other room. "Do you really believe that, David?" she finally asked.

Not really, the odds are against it, isn't your person anchored in your brain cells after all—I closed my eyes so tightly that I saw whirling flashes of light as of fireworks. Then again, why not, why try our little bits-and-pieces frame of reference on the real reality? How lovely it would be if there is love, sense, in the universe, if on this one score things are better and happier than we expect. Than we deserve? But it is too much to deserve for anyone, for the greatest saint, and at the same time, why would anyone be born to fear and misery?

I kicked my shoes off and lay beside her, outside the cover. There is but a limited number of us, a limited number of destinies and emotions; if you draw lines between them all, then that pattern is everything, all fates on this earth, and if you can grasp the pattern, you know all there is for us to know about human life.

"Don't people think with their heads?" Beatrix asked. "Then how can you think when your head is gone? How can you *be*?"

I said it was all a mystery and she was please not to worry about it.

"You know what, David," she said, "I think there's nothing. I'm scared." And she hid her face and started to cry again.

I hugged her. "If there is nothing else, then that's the better reason to make the most of it for everyone, to be as brave as Jean was. You and I, I mean. Let's be tough. Things are as they are. Some you can change, some you can't do anything about."

David Lum the philosopher. But what else was there to say?

Beatrix whispered a question I could not hear. I held my head closer to hers.

"If mommy has a grave," was what she was saying, "I want to put flowers on her grave."

"Jean has a grave. It is under water. But we will put flowers on it."

She made me promise.

"Jean has a monument," I said, "as good as the Arc de Triomphe. Exegi monumentum aere perennius! You know what that means?"

She shook her head without showing her face.

"It means, I have built a monument more durable than bronze. Bronze is very hard, like steel. It means that the real monuments are from what you do, and they cannot fall down. Ever. Exegi monumentum—they're verses, in Latin. Aren't they beautiful?"

But all I could hear from Beatrix's muttered answer was, "I don't understand them."

Those words filled me with a sudden despair.

72.

I DROVE HER to the airfield at Orient Point on the far tip of Long Island, a long drive and a silent one too, as Beatrix had announced that "no one" was to speak to her on the way.

I knew a man there from my LaGuardia days, Ned Reedy, and I had called him and reserved their air taxi. I also told him why I wanted it. When we arrived they had already brought it out, it was standing in front of the hangar, a little thing trembling in the wind coming in over the Sound.

The time was noon. The day did not look very friendly, dark clouds chased across the sky and the water was like lead.

"I suggest you two have something to eat," Ned said, "It's very rough now but the wind is dying down. I'll come and get you in a while."

"All right, that's sensible," I answered, but Beatrix pulled me aside. "I don't want anyone else to be there," she whispered urgently. "Please not. You said you were a pilot yourself! You musn't always fool me."

"I wasn't fooling you, I never said that! I used to work in a control tower, where you look at planes, you don't fly them. And I said I'd had some lessons once—Anyway, if I could fly that plane, I still couldn't take you, I'm responsible for you."

"Oh merde!" she cried. "You sound like my daddy. When he is afraid, that's what he says. *I'm* responsible for me."

I told Ned we would wait for him in the canteen. I had bought a wreath, and Beatrix had made her own, a strange-looking bouquet of yellow tulips which she had tied into a circle with ribbons. She now said she had to be by herself, and carrying her flowers, a notebook, and a shopping bag she had brought, she went out. In the doorway she turned around and gave me a lopsided smile. "I know you are never afraid, David," she said, for some reason suddenly in a heavily French accent.

Actually, she was wrong there: I had stopped my flying not for lack of money as I think I had told her, but because I was informed I'd never learn. I do not like machines, I do not even like cars, and at the controls of a Piper Cub I froze and had to fight the temptation to just push the stick forward and get the thing back on or even into the ground.

After a while I went out to look for Beatrix but she was nowhere to be seen. I decided not to worry. It was very quiet there; Orient Point is no tourist attraction on a blowy February day.

It was nearly two o'clock when Ned reappeared and said it wasn't getting any better and we might as well go. We walked to the plane. Holding my wreath, I tried out the right-hand door which was the type hinging all the way up, for people who go hunting from the air. "You're not going to keep that open," Ned said, "not in this weather." Beatrix came running, carrying her tulips and two packages, and we took off.

We made the regulation circuit and headed for Block Island. The plane shook a bit; I tapped Beatrix on her shoulder and she nodded to show she was fine, holding a finger against her lips to remind me of our no-talking agreement.

It was less than half an hour to Block Island, and then I made Ned turn north another six miles, after which he was to fly a circle with the island as its center. You could see us drift in the high wind. No other plane seemed to be in the sky and no boats at all on the water. I guessed Jean to have gone down north-northeast of Block Island, or that was a reasonable assumption anyway. It was better to sound certain and precise with Beatrix.

I was not fine. I could not stop myself from shaking and my shirt stuck to my back. I thought then that we were precisely in Jean's wake, the wake of that fatal flight of hers, and that the forces which had doomed her would now make me and her daughter perish, thus finally ending any remembrance of hers. I felt like a man looking down an abyss, both afraid and tempted to let himself fall, and when the wing tips vibrated I was waiting for them to break.

Clouds were amassing on the western horizon but the wind had blown the sky clear where we were, and I could see New England on my left and a light dot which was Block Island in the dark sea on my right. Then we had Block Island just behind the right wing. I tapped Beatrix on her shoulder once more and pointed down at the water.

She gave me a strange, sweet smile, and nodded. In that moment I got the better of my hysterics. We had followed Jean's path and we had made it and would go on from there. I signaled Ned to descend and he spiraled down until we were so low that I could see each wave and the fluorescence of seaweed or perhaps it was oil just below the surface. He lowered the flaps as if for a landing and cut back the power; against the wind we must have looked as if we were standing still. I put my hand on the door and looked at him; he shrugged which I took to mean, "Oh, okay," and pushed it up until it banged into its catch.

Immediately the feeling of the flight changed. We were no longer onlookers in an insulated glass cage, we became part of the scene. The wind burst in, tore the map off Ned's lap and out of the door, and a sharp smell of salt water wiped out the warmth and the oiliness of the cabin air. Beatrix looked around happily. She motioned for me to be first and I took my wreath and tossed it out. It landed much farther off than I had expected and vanished from our sight.

She now held her hand up, very solemnly. She opened one of her parcels and brought out a bottle with a letter in it which she threw far out and forward. We saw it hit the water and bob around. I do not know what was in the next parcel, for she threw it out unopened, and it sank. She kissed her tulips and waved at Ned to go still lower, but he shook his head. He banked, though, in a right turn, and as she threw her flowers, they fell slowly and reached the water of the Sound without breaking apart.

Ned wanted to shut the door, but she held his arm and shouted, "Please go around some more."

And so we circled over that yellow fleck of color on the water, below which, somewhere, lay not Jean but what now remained of her and of her plane and of the explosives turned into mush, and of her leaflets, still readable perhaps but not ever to be read. We were as if circling around an axis or perhaps an arrow, an imaginary arrow pointing at the sky, a pretend arrow, as Beatrix would have called it. I could see Jean's plane on the bottom of the sea and beside us in the air.

73.

"WILL YOU PHONE Andy for me?" Beatrix asked.

That was Andrew Highsmith. She would not say why. I dialed the number and when he answered, I told him to hold it and gave her the receiver. "Hello Andy," she said and then whispered to me, "Do you mind, David, for a moment?" and waved me out of the room. I obeyed, closed the door behind me, and started to wash our cups to show I was not eavesdropping.

Then she came running out of the room and gave me a piece of paper on which she had printed in careful capitals, "CARLA LIEBOWITZ." "Mommy's trail," she announced. "The trail that was cold, the scouts said."

She had asked Highsmith the name of that only other person who had been on Jean's side in the vote, "the person with her hand up." First he had answered that he did not remember, "but I just told him, 'Yes, you do,' and then he did. Very simple, David.—He doesn't know where she lives."

Simple enough, indeed. I knew that vote story had made a great impression on her, she must have visualized her mother in that room with just one supporter against all. It would have been like something she had been through, at her school or with the Garrison clan.

And thus Beatrix closed the last gap. There were not even that many Liebowitzes in the directory, and one of the *C*'s got us Carla. Carla Liebowitz of 242 West 112th Street told us that Jean and she had started visiting, after work, all the women in the fuel rod section of that plant and some of the men, those whom they knew to have spoken up against the lack of safety. It had been an endless drag, she said. "Imagine driving to all those little Jersey towns, and then they're not home, they're busy, they ask, 'Who sent you,' and on and on and on, for months. They're all scared of somebody, they rather have cancer, we might as well be living in Russia. It was a dud."

This had been for Jean's plan to stop the work, a plan for which inside help was needed. Carla did not know or did not want to say more about it. "What's the diff," she asked, "It was a nonstarter." Then what? Then Jean had come up with the airplane mission.

"She read us a letter by a man called De Bosis, and we said we would help."

Here Carla stopped and asked Beatrix, "Look, kid, you mind going in the other room and watching some TV while I talk to your daddy?"

Beatrix and I smiled at each other. She said, "Well, actually, I would mind. But if—"

"She can stay," I said hastily. "She knows everything. She must know everything."

"Okay," Carla said. The "we" to help had been she, Carla, and "a couple of guys." One had taken care of the printing (but after the plane accident he had asked her not to call him any more).

"That was no accident," Carla said. "No?"

"No. Yes. It was no accident."

Another man had promised to handle the most tricky business, he was going to get gelignite or some stuff like it. "I don't even know if he did," she said. "By then Jean had decided that there would be no more horizontal contact between us so to speak, but only with her, you see. For security. Of course we did what she said. It was her—her show." ("Her life," she was going to say.) "That's all I know. At about that time, she vanished from her apartment, on West 12th Street. Next thing I read in the paper, well, you know. —I work for the SHAD Alliance now, an antinuke group."

"Who is the gelignite man?" I asked.

"What's jellynite?" Beatrix asked.

Carla hesitated. "What is it?" Beatrix asked urgently.

"An explosive. Like dynamite?" And to me she said, "I'm sure you're on the level, but still. You understand. Give me your phone number, and I'll ask him to call you. That way it's up to him."

I agreed, but he never called.

There seemed no reason to pursue it. Say his name is Anthony Lum, or David Chase, or Alfred Garrison the Tenth. What's the diff?

Now all of Jean's life is known to us, or all even Beatrix and I are allowed to know.

74.

I took Beatrix to P.S. 41 and told the admissions lady we had just come back to Jane Street from Angola, and I had no documents at all but my daughter Beatrix— Beatrix Chase—belonged in the fifth grade. No documents at all? She would have to discuss that, we were to come back in two days.

That was fine with us. "What a dirty place," Beatrix said before she had even closed the door of the office behind us. She had been all set to be in school that day and now we both felt inordinately relieved. It was an unexpected vacation.

"Where shall we go?" I asked. "It's your party."

"Can I really say?"

"Absolutely."

"I want to see mommy's flying school."

That wiped the smile off my face, but she was a strong-willed girl, a daughter of her mother, and she seemed to have accepted the idea with a vengeance that everything her mother had done made sense, and was therefore not to be regretted or mourned.

Seeing the place again made me shiver. My old office was locked, with a sign on the door, "Please apply at the canteen, on the west side of the field." We drove over to the canteen, and there the counter woman put down those paper placemats with airplanes all over them for us and said, "Yes, folks?" "Don't you recognize me?" I asked. "Sure,

you were the office guy, Lum. How've you been?" "Fine,"
I said. Well, and thanks for the enthusiastic reception.

"What about the school?" I asked. "It says, 'Apply at the
canteen.' "

"Yeah. Well, you know, winter—Benson will be here if
you want him."

"When?"

She looked over her shoulder at that clock. "Oh, I dunno,
any time now."

I hesitated.

"I know he got news from Joseph," she said.

So we waited. Beatrix brought out her notebook and
wrote what looked like a letter, concentrating hard, with
her tongue out of her mouth. At one point she started to ask
me, "How do you spell—?" but then said, "Never mind."

After two coffees, one milkshake, and three Cokes, we decided to give up on Benson. When I paid, the counter
woman said, "Give me your phone number, why don't you.
He may have something for you, maybe he knows of a job."

I thought she wanted to make up for having been unfriendly and I gave her the number. "It's in the name of
Chase," I said. That was a great mistake.

On the way home Beatrix announced, "I've got a letter
for you." She handed me a sheet of paper all folded up, and
climbed into the back seat while I undid it with one hand.

I read, "Why did you say, Jean has not lost her war?

"Why did you say, we will win?

"She did not bomb the enemy. Did she?

"You always fool me. I am not a child."

I looked at her in the rearview mirror, but she was staring out of the window, shielding her face with her hands.

That night I sat on her bed and told her, no, I had not
been fooling her, she'd see I had not. Jean had not got to
the enemy, true, but she had set the sights for all of us.
"You'll see," I said.

75.

WE HAD A SPLENDID DAY following that one. First we drove by the Royalton Hotel for my mail and I found a letter with a job offer at the FAA control center in Aurora, Illinois. April 15. "In just about two months," I told Beatrix.

"And then I can leave the Black Hole again?"

"Absolutely."

"The Black Hole" had become her designation for P.S. 41.

On the strength of that news we decided to go everywhere and to spend money like mad.

"Let's start with going up the highest building," she asked.

Does it need explaining why it would be festive for a man of thirty-nine to go sightseeing and having lunch and dinner with a girl of just ten? It is not odd if she is his daughter and I am sure we had as much going for us along those lines as most fathers-children. And there was my role as a substitute father-plus-mother, our joint adventure, all sorts of things. We both knew that the future with or without new job was uncertain, but that day we did not mind. "We are tough, aren't we," Beatrix stated several times.

Of course Beatrix looked like Jean and even more like Jean in Chicago, but there was nothing subterranean about it all, or if there was, it was so very *sub* that I never knew. I simply mean we were not Lolita-ing together. I felt tender toward that little girl with her courage and her spindly arms, but I did not confuse her with Jean. She made Jean real.

In the World Trade Center I bluffed my way up to the dining room where we gazed out of the windows and then quickly left without looking the maitre d' in the face, and we went to the zoo and we had tea in the Palm Court of the Plaza which was a gyp but pleased her because it was like the Ritz in Paris, she said, where she had once walked through but her father had forbidden her to sit down. Why they had walked through it, she did not remember. We came out on Fifth Avenue in the dusk of a winter's day, with all the lights, under the rapidly withdrawing midnight-blue sky, and she said, "Oh, this is a lovely town, isn't it, David?"

It was.

The next morning, when we reported in the admission office of P.S. 41 at the appointed time, a policewoman was sitting on the windowsill and I thought nothing of it.

The school lady shuffled her papers, looked at the police-woman, at me, and asked, "Is your real name David Lum?" And before I even had the chance to say no, two men came in. One handed me a document and the other told me to hold up my arms, and frisked me. Beatrix turned very pale and then started to cry.

"Never you mind, honey," the policewoman said, coming over to her. "You're going home to your daddy."

Beatrix stared at her and screamed, "I don't want to, I don't want to!" That was the last thing I heard her say as the men rushed me out of there.

"Don't worry! I'll get you back!" I shouted before they could close the door.

I was charged with kidnap under Title 18, Paragraph 1201, "willfully transporting a person in interstate or foreign commerce," "decoying or enticing a minor away from its parents" and more stuff like that. The lawyer who showed up in my cell implied I was lucky there was no death penalty for my crimes, but when I had been in court and talked to the judge, a black lady who did not interrupt, she set trial for May 25 next and released me on a hundred-dollar bail bond.

Beatrix had gone, though, she had been flown to Paris on the day itself of my arrest, in the custody of a special bailiff paid for by Garrison (who had got us because the word had been out at the flying school). It was the judge who informed me of that, adding that any effort of mine to contact the child would be considered contempt of court—"And that," she said, "is very costly indeed with me, Mr. Lum."

76.

IN A SECONDHAND BOOKSTORE on Fourth Avenue I once found a book announcing on its title page that it described "all events since Creation." It had been printed in the year 1770 in London and the price written in it was only five dollars. In it were all buildings, all mountains, all statues, all parks, all cities, listed as if everything was fixed for all time and would not change any further.

I was about to buy it when I saw that it also listed "all miracles since Creation" and these turned out to be the burning bush of Moses but also chicken eggs on record as having hatched homunculi, little men, and a goat with three heads born in a small German town, where the air already would have smelled of the burned flesh of tortured witches. It made me feel uneasy and the drawing of an egg with a homunculus in it was especially revolting. I put the book back in its place. All events since creation. In the system of things, our thinking will end up with considerable fewer (manmade) years than the total flying time put in by the archaeopteryx.

Shores of bright lights. A song about a café in Yucatan, "with a large, slow-moving fan." A pleasant image, half–Joseph Conrad, half–old foreign-legion movie. A silly rhyme. But texts and names of music are harboring a romantic world, a vanished world. "Nights in the Gardens of Spain," that was a record of mine, long since lost in one of my many moves, which I would play ad infinitum. A lakeshore or a coastline at dusk with lights flickering through a blueish haze has a meaning, as if here nature and mankind had for a moment combined in creating something like a new species, a new experience of nostalgia and melancholy and happiness.

I do not know where I had that from, I've never seen such a sight. The New Jersey shore with the Palisades Amusement Park surely does not qualify. But that image stands for "the other life" which I might have chosen, a sensual and unserious but happy life, with no thought of "all events since Creation." A life I could still choose. Or maybe only if I had lived, say, just one generation earlier.

The manager of an American Army PX in West Germany, one December in the late 1960s, had made a special effort on his Christmas display, he had built a crèche of greens and colored candies, with little Jesus and the ox and the ass, and for non-Christian GI's a table-long Peace and Happy Holidays tableau with candles, ribbons, bottles of wine and perfume and cranberry sauce. A German student who was in the PX (where he did not have the right to enter) was shook up by the discordance between this and the sets in the television and radio department of the store where at news time you saw six Marines on six sets set fire to six villages. The student set fire to the Christmas display.

He did not do much damage. The German race over-reacts, however; officials who had once in the Wehrmacht or the Party discussed the obliterations of cities reacted like

Quaker ministers to this violence, and he was hunted as a dangerous animal. There is a parallel here to the case of Jean More. The student, whose name was Baader, became or was made into a terrorist, and he would soon be dead, with several others.

To be killed without having perpetrated violence is nobler, more disinterested, above all more respectful of human life. In one word: safer. Men feel safer with the passion of Jesus than with the passion of Baader or with the passion of Suleiman Alepin which lasted twenty times as long. The *Petit Larousse* in the major's office in Suresnes said that General Jean-Baptiste Kléber had been killed "by a fanatic." And indeed, who was to say that Suleiman Alepin had not been just a crazy kid, and the same obviously for Baader, and all the others? Any Westchester psychiatrist could explain their deeds within the allotted fifty minutes, and did that not mean that courage did not enter into it?

Manmade years. Why are years manmade? Because only men and women have measured that time in which the earth revolves from one point in its ellipse to the same point, and only they have written down the laws of that harmony, laws not really understandable at all but beautiful in their symmetry. It is not nature which abhors a vacuum but human beings. Still, perhaps there is truly and outside our imaginations a music of the spheres, playing through another aether.

Whether there is or not, I admire the courage of such human measurings, out into darkness.

Courage is a characteristic I have of late been most preoccupied with. Not, I hope, because I basically lack it. I don't think I do. What preoccupies me is an awareness of new qualifications and new reservations cropping up all the time when I try to define what would be admirable about it.

77

I HAD TO MAKE a choice. It was time to get with it. Choosing is my weakest spot.

I had held out so long that now I did not have much to show for myself. I had no illusions about that, I was an assistant air traffic controller if and when employed, with a lot of inappropriate quiz-program-type general education on the side. I could be considered a misfit but then, so must Lauro de Bosis, not to mention Alepin or Princip. I was just the right material to be the subject of one of those little items on page fifty-nine of the second section of the paper where somebody has done something crazy.

When the judge set me free, I went straight back to our Jane Street apartment. It looked much the same. The cups from the breakfast that Beatrix and I had had before walking to P.S. 41 were in the sink; she must have put them there when the cops brought her back to collect her possessions. Beatrix had drawn a heart in soap on the bathroom mirror and put the original photograph of Jean (with the writing on the back) on the pillow in the bedroom. That was all that was left by her. She had kept the key, which we had hung around her neck with a piece of string in a solemn ceremony (her first key), on what we had thought would be her first New York school day. It was not an item she would have forgotten; it was her way of saying she meant to be back, I was sure of that. The unspent part of the money was still in the sock where we had hid it. She would never tell her father of the savings account, it was our best secret. I aired the place; it had become musty during my arrest days.

Sitting in front of the open window which looked out on the roof of chimneys, rusty aerials, and halfway down the block an orangy cat chewing on what seemed to be a dead pigeon, I took out Jean's leaflet with its letter to me typed on the back. I had kept it in my diary, folded in four—luckily, or it would have stayed behind in my suitcase in the Austerlitz depot.

I reread, "The world is poisoned out of existence in a hundred different ways," and how the writer was scattering her message over the town of Providence, home of Alson-McDonald, and how she would crash her plane into their headquarters, her way of "paying for the television time and the newspaper space." Signed, "An American Woman." The first enemy plane in the sky of the United States.

I got out a pad and a pen, I was going to redraft this. No harm in trying out how it would read. So I shifted those words around, "A friend of mine who was employed . . ." and things like that, and signing, "An American." It did not sound right at all.

Then I thought to myself, Christ no, of course not, I'm not going to change this, if they are used, they have to be used as they are, for and on behalf of Jean and in her place! And then I also felt I could do it and, who knows, might do it.

How to get those leaflets printed again? I did not know anyone I could confide them to. Presumably commercial printers proofread their stuff without bothering to think about what they read, and then again perhaps they do bother.

I left the apartment and hurried up the avenue to a photocopy shop, and had them make one copy of the leaflet. There is an overgrown, walled little space at the corner of Jane Street and I sat on that wall and studied the Xerox. It was fine. You could just see where the original had been folded but it did not matter. The leaflet also had a stain from when it had been in my refrigerator in the frozen crabmeat carton, and on the copy the stain had come out as a gray blob, somewhat in the shape of a starfish. That did not matter either, on the contrary, it was a seal of authenticity: Jean, her mark.

I chased up a Yellow Pages out of one of the closets in the apartment and telephoned places renting duplicating machines. The following morning they delivered an electrostat copier at a rental of eighty dollars a week, with ten thousand sheets of the special paper needed to go with it.

In the typewriter room of the 42nd Street library I had typed at the bottom of the leaflet: "This message was written by Jean More, who did not carry out her plan because her plane was sabotaged. It was sabotaged by Alson-McDonald before takeoff. She crashed into Block Island Sound. Alson-McDonald killed her twice over, which is perhaps a principle of nuclear arms anyway."

78.

THE COPIER WAS STANDING on the floor: the table was too rickety for it. After trying all sorts of setups, this had shown itself the most practical one, with me beside it on a couple of pillows to keep feeding in the paper and pressing the button.

It was dark outside now. The machine produced an acrid smell which I hoped was not a sign it was about to burn out. I kept getting up, opening the window for fresh air and closing it again when it got too cold. The pile of leaflets done was still painfully small.

I had not been prepared for this snag: the machine could do only three hundred copies an hour. Then, according to the instructions, it needed to cool off for ten to fifteen minutes. At that rate, ten thousand leaflets would take almost forty hours of running the thing. Even so, ten thousand —that was one-fortieth of the DeBosis/Jean More operation. But those sheets of paper cost forty dollars a thousand.

I thought it was better to keep going as long as I could, rather than work a number of hours a day. If I did it that way, the whole business would begin to appear ludicrous; I had to keep at it without more navel gazing. I had started at noon, with a supply of potato chips and sandwiches from the delicatessen, and I made a pot of instant coffee whenever the machine took its rest.

At about two in the morning I unplugged it and went to sleep. Fourteen hours minus the pauses: some three thousand leaflets should have been done. I surely did not consider starting to count them but I could see it was less than that.

I woke up before it was even light, and got into my clothes without washing or shaving. The street was filled with a murky light, a bad mixture of nature and electricity. The early traffic raced up the avenue in a way which was reckless and listless at the same time, they were going so fast not because they felt vigorous but because they didn't give a damn. I could tell from their faces when they came to a halt at the traffic light on my corner. It depressed me, this street and this avenue, and it was hard not to give up right then. I did not, I closed the window again and drew the curtain, I was going to shut out the world and run my machine in seclusion. A French Resistance operation, while outside the Gestapo in one of those trucks with slit windows circles the block and tries to get a bearing on me. No, that's for radio transmitters. Perhaps they had something like that to trace the rumble of a printing press. Or the peculiar smell of this copy machine, that should be easy. It is a race what will get me first, they bursting in with submachine guns, or the fumes of the copy machine, or these awful

[197]

potato chips with their "stabilizers, anti-oxidants, and permitted amounts of CB 20." CB 20?

79.

THE SOUND PRINT of New York City through the day must be as identifiable as a man's fingerprints. How familiar every noise is and how much it is of my time, part of me, totally mysterious to my great-grandfather, or to Alepin the Cairo gardens assassin. He lives in a world of birds singing (I assume Cairo has them although I would not know which species, hieroglyphics are full of birds), of muezzins if that is the proper word chanting from minarets, of street vendors: the more pliable noise from a world without engines.

How does he see this world? He is a student of theology, I remember; what does this Egyptian theology look like? Does he feel the earth standing still, with the stars as holes pricked in the firmament? No, surely not, ten centuries ago Egypt already had those wise Arab and Jewish astronomers, Ben this and Ibn that claculating eclipses. The planetarium runs a program on them. What then? Is he lost in a staggering infinity like I am?

I have opened the sixth of the ten packs of paper, I am over halfway. The smelly copier has started making noises too, now, a special electric kind of bird song. I can only hope I'm not ruining the thing. Still, it is probably not even worth more than the eighty dollars they charge for a week's use, payable in advance. The leaflets still come out looking pretty smart, with their mysterious almost invisible cross where the folds had changed the texture or the reflection factor or whatever it is of the paper in the original. The Stouffer crabmeat stain, reaching what for a stain must be akin to immortality, has by now already been reproduced more than five thousand times. And I am half-groggy, half-high on instant coffee and what I hope is vodka—I found a bottle about one-fourth full under the kitchen sink. Maybe it is stuff to clean the toilet bowl.

Five thousand "An American Woman." Jean, you will not regret that rainy Haymarket evening when a scruffy man, old enough to be your father, offered his help. The blood on his shirt (which inspired confidence in you and your friend) was innocent, that is to say, he, I, was just a victim who had been punched in the nose and not remotely an actor in that particular drama or in any other drama. I was just a bloody onlooker as they would say in England, a bloodied onlooker. Always have been, before and since.

No more, when I started this machine all was changed. Vicarious living ended.

Violence, the physical bending of fate, is no longer something I contemplate in my books or watch on a screen to forget my real problems such as a ruined marriage or a toothache. No, I have made fate my real problem! I, David Chandler Lum, a person so typical or so untypical that I have so far left no monument on this earth but the fifth digit in an election return or the point zero two in the population density of Queens.

But what am I thinking of, I am not running off these leaflets to advertise myself. I am advertising Beatrix, advertising children whose body cells are not to be attacked by alpha, beta, or gamma rays or particles, I forget which is which. It may be misdirected or pointless. Ten years, a hundred years, what's the diff, as Carla says.

Nevertheless, every time I push this button and every sheet of paper which comes out, make me feel good for a second.

I have stared at this machine for nearly two days and only now do I see it has a name, in black plastic letters; I had thought they were some kind of decorative curlicues. Once I have seen it, I do not understand how I could have failed to perceive that those are letters. The machine is called the Monivox. Or maybe that x is a fancy z and it is the Monivoz. What sort of name is that? Surely the brain product of someone in the mysterious East, for this machine was assembled in Singapore where women put the parts together and ruin their eyes at a dime an hour. Their turn will come. When Alson-McDonald, not least though Jean's, and my, and Beatrix's war, moves from Providence to Singapore, those wages will go up to fifteen cents at least. Ha ha.

I don't feel clever with such thoughts, I don't want to keep myself awake with them. I am pretty certain that Alepin does not think of the political status of Egypt or the economic influence of France while planning his murder. He has dark thoughts, thoughts of blood and hate and love.

Those are the thoughts I want to have, to keep me from falling back down into the place reserved for a near middle-aged assistant air traffic control fellow expected on April 15 in Aurora.

Another night, and another morning.

80.

A GOOD OMEN. At the Royalton they had a picture post-card for me from Beatrix. Also a letter from the major.

Beatrix's picture did not show the Eiffel Tower but a nest of kittens. That was her kind of irony, though not all-the-way irony: she would have thought they were sweet. Her card said, "Keep the homefires burning, David." (That is from an old war song I had taught her and which we sang together while driving along.) "He can't keep me long. Vive notre guerre. Love. Jean." ("Homefires" read "home-fries," but certainly not as a joke. She often transposed the letters in a word.)

The major—to get a letter from him was a surprise. He started out gentlemanly by saying he would have liked the chance to offer me a farewell drink and thus I was forbidden to pay back those few francs I owed him for a bar bill. And then he continued:

"About war. De bello civili. I am not as much of a die-hard as you think. When I speak of war, I leave the exchange of nuclear rockets out of my consideration. We do not know what such an exchange means, we are as ignorant of it in our hearts, in our guts, as those red-uniformed French *chasseurs* were of high explosives in August 1914. They all died. We would all die. It is a matter very far beyond the competence not only of generals but also of politicians. In a more pious age, it would be a matter of religion. Let us say it is a matter of teleology. The existence of man. No one should dare discuss it except those concerned, i.e. every single one of us, the people. With that word I certainly do not mean our ill-chosen, ill-mannered, ill-tempered but forever smiling so-called representatives. I mean it literally: everyone. If everyone agrees to end it all, well, then so be it.

"War, in the sense in which it interests me as a phenomenon of human courage and endeavor, will henceforth be civil war and regional war. Of course you will interject, 'Major, it has never beeen anything else.' " (I would not have interjected that at all. He liked to turn his speeches into seeming dialogues.)

"You may also be pleased to hear that I have given

thought to your words about true courage remaining unknown; 'secret' I think you said.

"You talked to me about that fellow in Egypt who killed
General Kléber. Between parentheses, I don't know why
you were so obsessed by the case. Kléber was a mediocre
general, and the French were presently to be forced into
withdrawal from Egypt anyway.

"However that may be, you deserve that I put in writing to you a thought I have never entertained before. Perhaps *we* have to be the underdogs, the natives, for a generation or two before we can start writing history objec-
tively, and before we dare compare the assassin's dagger in
the night with the cavalry charge at high noon."

Well—I read all this in the Royalton coffee shop, with
half an eye on my car parked outside. That was certainly
a good letter.

I liked the major. I was even comforted by his words although I was not completely sure what kind of message he
was sending me. But he belonged to that rare species of
people who somehow make you want to earn their approval,
and I had visualized him picking up one of my leaflets from
the street and reading it with a frown of displeasure.

81.

I POUNDED THE STREETS of New York while in Jane
Street those stacks of leaflets were sitting on the floor of the
bedroom (I would wake up in the night, turn on the light
and read one, although I surely knew those words by heart
now. Beatrix's card with "Long live our war" was stuck in
the mirror).

I walked to clear my head, and my ideas fluctuated and meandered. On one street corner the city and with the city, life itself, would seem so pleasing and simple that the man who had Xeroxed those leaflets was a stranger to me, and a maniac too. On the next corner a wind might rise and blow about the dirt, overturn the bag of a black woman sitting on the sidewalk, her face not black but gray really, and she would mutter curses at God knows whom. That was a leaflet corner.

Think of all those thousands and thousands of men, as average and as quiet as I, sitting in the trenches of France, at dawn the officer blows his whistle, they climb out and get themselves shot dead. Two out of three. Most of those men have a lot going for them, their wives or girls have not been killed before them but are waiting at home, rosy and healthy, thinking of them as they look at themselves naked.

I found myself at 50th Street and Broadway and walked over to the East Side, keeping my eyes on that strange triangular top of Citibank which is like an ancient, Pharaonic monument. I was on my way to visit the massage parlor. But when I was lying on that slightly greasy table, the idea that had brought me there, to have at least one more coming before I might, maybe, get myself killed in a plane, froze me. No matter how hard the Puerto Rican lady pulled, nothing happened. "You're much tired," she said. "Wait."

A minute later another woman came in, half as old and half as fat. I thought, I'm not going to waste my money; and deciding right then I was not going on any plane rides, I got my concentration back and functioned properly.

But on Third Avenue, before I could change my mind, I telephoned Ned at Orient Point and said I was going to take up flying lessons again. He hesitated but then answered, "All right. I won't be here tomorrow. Day after tomorrow. At twelve?" Twelve was fine.

With another week's unemployment money, I had eighty-two dollars left. I kept twelve for gas and tolls to get there, and for the remaining seventy I got more Xerox paper. It should have bought seventeen hundred and fifty sheets, but they gave me two thousand.

82.

IN THE LAST TWILIGHT, Lauro de Bosis landed unharmed on the sea when he had run out of gas. The evening was calm, the Mediterranean just barely rocked the plane. It would stay afloat for a while. To the east he thought he could see light reflected against the clouds, the lights of Rome. There, his four hundred thousand leaflets had now been set on their unstoppable course. He smiled.

Why doesn't life imitate the movies, why couldn't De Bosis have been picked up by a movie producer's yacht or just by a Greek tramp steamer? He wasn't, he drowned.

More important even, did he until his last conscious moment live happily or at least at peace with what he had done?

Is it possible in the agony of drowning to see oneself as a poetic hero living out an idea? Was De Bosis that strong, that naive, that romantic, that while conscious he had no regrets, no sense of futility?

It is not difficult to imagine oneself in his place once the engine had died.

I am sitting in the open cockpit or maybe out on the wing, in the soft silence, the wind on my face, a setting turning from blue to quickly darkening purple, peaceful if it were not for that fatality of the slow sinking of the plane, not more than an inch a minute yet. I can just gauge it on the row of bolts along the nose, there were eleven of them above water before, now only nine.

I know I must understand De Bosis. I have to understand him right now, while lying in my bed in Jane Street, not when I myself am dying and when it will be too late. I want to know if there is a terrible bitterness to be tasted of ultimate regret, of not knowing "how it will end" or worse, regret of not having put one's own life before everything else.

Then again I imagine that De Bosis is to be envied. He, not Jean. He had not known he had failed. Jean had known.

The plane goes under, the nose with the engine first. De Bosis has long taken off his leather jacket and his boots. The water is not cold, he can hope to stay alive for another hour. But he would not have struggled or even hoped, for had he not written at the top of his last letter, "The story of my death"? He knew how it would be. Surely a poet has that much insight, and I believe he would have dropped the letter in the French mailbox with a strange satisfaction, with a feeling of *joining*.

I am not sure what I mean with that, the word just came to me.

Perhaps then Jean had not been bitter either. Perhaps during those last moments at the dead controls, her consciousness about to end forever, she had not wasted one precious second on Alson-McDonald and her leaflets. Perhaps she too had had that same sensation of joining, as Lauro de Bosis had when his hand touched the metal of the mailbox at the airport of Marseilles.

83.

I SLEPT, I woke up in a sweat, went to look for a sleeping pill, and sank back into a kind of stupor. I had dreams which were not really dreams for I chose the subjects. At the same time I imagined I would learn something about the future from them.

I made love with Jean or almost, in a genuine dream. Afterward I tried to keep her, have her answer me.

In the black center of the night I was so tired that tiredness became the human condition, that nothing further was to be expected on earth, nothing good, nothing bad even, there was no reason for the continuation of people looking into one another's faces, or at the sky, or for touching one another's bodies, for thinking, for tasting, for enjoying their brief advantage over the lieutenant in the Hispano-Suiza and the private from Steamboat Springs whose mortal remains now tremble with the truck traffic on Avenue Woodrow Wilson, Suresnes, France. A very brief advantage. One beat in time. But then I woke up completely and did not understand this feeling any more.

I got up, stood under the shower for about an hour, and dressed very neatly. I walked down the stairs, checking again and again that I had my apartment keys and had not locked myself out, and got the car.

I owned only one suitcase now, and I had to go up to the apartment and down three times with it before all the leaflets, twelve thousand of them, were in the trunk. No wrapping paper was to be found in any of the closets, but I had one dollar to spare, to buy some on the Island on my way to Orient Point.

I drove to First Avenue, and across the Triboro Bridge just as the sun came up right in front of me.

84.

NED REEDY now clearly remembered what I had once told him about my flying efforts, and he looked very puzzled. Still, he did not object, he only said, "If you're sure, kid. At least it's a nice day."

He took me up in a Piper Tomahawk and it was the same as before. When he let go of the controls, I froze in my seat and for fear of pushing the thing into the ground, I pulled so hard on the column that the plane sat up on its tail and buffeted as if in a sudden storm. Ned knocked my hands away and pushed forward. "You nearly got us stalled there," he said, "and in this machine, that takes talent."

"Sorry."

"Okay."

"Show me the whole routine, Ned," I asked. "Perhaps I'll just watch this time, and refresh my memory."

When he had us back on the ground, I said, "You let me sit here a while and get a bit familiar with it all, and after lunch we can try again. If you're free."

"I'm free all right. I'll be free from now till Easter. But maybe you're wasting your money."

I shrugged and he got out and went into his office.

After a few minutes I got out too, went to my car, and opened the trunk. There were my leaflets, one huge bundle wrapped in brown paper. It was very heavy, but once I had it in my arms without it bursting open, I carried it to the plane in little steps and dropped it into Ned's seat. Then I got in again and fastened my seatbelt.

I closed my eyes and rehearsed the maneuver, started the engine and very slowly taxied to the center line of the runway. I could see the office in the rear mirror and there was no sign of Ned.

I opened the throttle and I rolled forward with a startling jolt; at the same moment the plane started to turn its head sideways. I got it straight, though, with the rudder, I cleared the sweat out of my eyes with my sleeve, and pulled at the column, very slightly, and then still more. The plane was flying, over the water of the Sound.

85.

I SHOOK LIKE A LEAF and could feel the sweat run down my back inside my shirt.

But I realized full well I was not *really* afraid any more, or if afraid, not paralyzed. I could breathe. My fears had been the fears of making a decision and that was past and done with. I assuredly could not land this thing anyway.

I even had time to wonder whether I should have mailed a postcard to Beatrix from the airfield and if so, what I should have said. There was a red mailbox beside the door of Ned's office, I had not focussed on it but I had the memory of that square of color.

No touching the throttle or the flaps, I had told myself: too fast was better than too slow. I did not want to look at the instruments either. I looked out of the window instead until the water was quite far below me, and again as slowly as in a dream I pushed the column forward until it was more or less what Ned had called "in neutral."

I had a car map in the left pocket of my jacket, and I let go of the column with one hand and got it out. Unfolding it with one hand was unnerving but it ended up in my lap at the proper fold, where I had drawn a line from Orient Point to Providence, just about forty-five degrees, northeast.

After a while I cleared my vision sufficiently to distinguish the compass. I knew of course there were all sorts of variations and corrections, I was after all an assistant air traffic controller, but I counted on Providence being big enough to show itself when I got anywhere near.

I managed to undo the wrapping around the leaflets in a series of hasty one-hand pulls.

There I was, high above; the sun had vanished but the sky was without clouds, a dome of amorphous haze, and I was already crossing the coastline of Connecticut. For a moment I felt marvelous, the joy natural flyers like Jean presumably feel. I even shed the idea that the engine would stop if I did not listen to it all the time. But then the lump in my throat was back; I think I was superstitiously afraid of not feeling bad. Rarely, one of the wingtips dipped but without giving me time to be very frightened for the plane righted itself somehow.

Now for the first time I became calm enough to see myself from a distance. Instead of struggling within that little cabin I asked myself what the people in ground control stations would make of it.

Did Providence have a computer with the flight plan of every single private plane and would they bother if I showed up on their screen? I knew the airport was on the south edge of the town and I would try to stay away from it as far as possible. Alson-McDonald headquarters was in the northern section of Providence, beyond the bend in the river. Would it really look from above as if seeing a map? I had no idea. Streets and roads never seem to when I am driving, but this would perhaps be easier.

The Tomahawk was glass all around, and the sky appeared to be absolutely empty. Far to the right and above me I saw a vapor trail such as jet planes make but when I blinked, it had vanished. I wondered if I should try and practice a turn here in all this clear space but decided

[209]

against it. Glancing at my watch I saw I had been in the air only twenty minutes. That was a shock. It had seemed a very long time. It should be less than an hour to the city, but then I did not know the wind and indeed, I could not grasp the meaning of the airspeed dial, if that was what I was looking at. I was not as clear-headed any more as when the plane was above water.

I got hold of my handkerchief and dried my hands one at a time and then my neck, and told myself, this is it, no more nonsense now. I'm going to think about Jean as hard as I can. It will help, not in some mystical way but through the feeling and the memory of that enormous calm of hers. I hate machines, and she was such a machine operative, a machine-wright. Wickedly, machines had been her undoing, but that was on another level. She worked well with things manufactured to fit within our lives. It is not such a jump from a Chinese kite to this little plane. Perhaps there is also a link from little planes and old cars to those new machines which ignore life, but if so it is a link I do not see. Nuclear machinery cannot but be built joylessly, it is literally untouchable, and the men who own it cannot but fail to understand it.

The haze up ahead and to the east of me along the horizon was changing color and was brownish instead of white. First I imagined this was the sign of some dreadful storm brewing but then I saw it was smoke. And not long thereafter the chopped-up and barren squares of winter field below me gave way to houses, with cars around them and running between them. I saw high-rises ahead. I was approaching Providence.

86.

AFTER THAT the peaceful times were over.

The two doors of the plane lock with an overhead latch. I had seen that when Ned opened it, but stupidly I did not let it sink in that the lock would obviously only operate when opening the doors from the outside, and I nearly broke my fingers feeling for it without looking.

Finally I found the proper catch on the door. My door opened slightly and fell shut, and the plane lurched badly. It seemed about an hour before it was quiet again but not the way it was before, it was clearly losing height. I pulled the column back a little, which produced a shudder, so I hastily undid that movement. I was wearing my desert boots, I managed to get the right one off without too much wriggling and after I got my door open a crack, I pushed the boot between the door and the plane wall to keep it open. It worked; the door hinged up front and the wind or the speed of the plane kept it in place, with a couple of inches space. The plane did not seem to mind.

Now I saw that somehow I had moved the throttle back during all this, and that was why I was not flying level. I pushed it forward and the plane started climbing.

Presently I crossed a freeway cutting through the city, which meant as I knew from the map that I was over the center. I let go of the steering column entirely and pushed a pack of leaflets out through the space between the door and the side of the cabin. A few blew back and into my face, but most of them vanished, and I pushed another batch through and another. I did not see any results but kept doing this, and suddenly I saw in my rear mirror what looked like snow: a dense cloud of leaflets descending on the town. Holy Jesus, it worked. Now I was out over open country again and I had to turn. When you turn a plane, you have to bank it, I knew that perfectly well, but did not dare try. I thought if I turned very, very slowly, I could do without the banking, and thus I turned the control to the left just half an inch at the time. I could see the ground below me and it did not turn, and I moved the wheel a bit faster.

Then the plane was yawing, like a sailboat, and my mind became blank, I lost all idea of what to do. Instead of clutching at anything I forced myself to let go. I loosened my seat belt and pushed all the remaining leaflets out through the crack, without focussing on my surroundings as there was a sickening sliding movement going on under my seat. And as I looked forward again, I saw right in front of me, perhaps two thousand feet away, that cement Alson-McDonald Eiffel Tower with the gold A-McD. It was sparkling as if a private sun concentrated its rays on it alone.

That instant, without bravery on my part, from within this weird, detached limbo I was now whirling in, waiting to hit something anyway, I shouted "Hurrah," and grabbed the control column back. I surely had not planned it, but I would crash this plane into horny Dan's top floor. A crazy anger, as if I could see the guy raping Jean on top of that roof; and now I remembered everything Ned had shown me, I gave aileron and rudder and flew straight, and I pointed the nose and made for the golden A-McD.

Heaven knows, there was nothing kamikaze-like about it, I did not have a thought left about myself, I was just pointing, it was like going to shoot the man. I never have shot anybody and had not thought I could, but something had worked loose in me and finally it seemed perfectly proper and natural to feel that much anger.

I do not know what I did wrong but I did not hit the A-McD building nor the tower. Suddenly again, they had completely disappeared from my view, and I was flying over the same freeway or one like it, with a gleam from the river on my left. I was so low that I could clearly distinguish the cars and trees and even people, and cars were stopping and people getting out to look up at me. Then unaccountably, the lower half of the windshield steamed over and as I leaned forward to wipe it clean I hit some gauge or control, and so hard that my hand started bleeding. In that second the engine stopped.

Sudden silence, and the rush of the wind past the open door. The plane was no longer a machine, well, in a way at least it was not, and I regained most control over myself. I saw below me, through the windshield which was all clear again, a park with a lot of lakes and streams. I pushed the control column, closed my eyes and banged my head, and the plane was sitting motionless in the middle of a pond.

I threw up or nearly. There was an awful burning taste in my mouth. My knees had gone wrong: my legs were pointing sideways but it did not hurt particularly. I tried to open the door wider but could not, and thought, I am going to drown now.

Then I saw a policeman who seemed to be standing right in the pond. He leaned over the wing, he rested his elbow on it which looked odd for the wing was under water. He opened the plane door on my side without any effort and eyed me.

"Are you hurt?" he asked.

"I think I broke my legs."

He did not appear in any hurry. "I'll call for an ambulance," he said. "And I guess you know there are about twenty-five violations I'm going to hit you with."

"That's all right, officer," I said.

"Who are you?"

That one moment was my first one of complete happiness since Jean had vanished, no, maybe it was the first one ever in my life, the first one since I had known who I was and had learned that when my mother screamed, "Dave," that was me. I smiled at the policeman and leaned over a bit to dip my bleeding hand in the water of the pond.

"I'm Lauro de Bosis," I said.

And he pulled out a pad to write it down.

HANS KONING was born Hans Koningsberger in Amsterdam, Holland. He left his country as a student to serve in the British Army during World War II, and in 1951 arrived in the United States by way of Indonesia. In 1958 the publication of his first novel, *The Affair*, set his reputation as an American writer. Since then he has written eight novels, including *A Walk with Love and Death, I Know What I'm Doing*, and *The Revolutionary*, for which he helped write and produce the film adaptations. Two nonfiction books, *Love and Hate in China* and *A New Yorker in Egypt*, grew out of his work as a reporter for *The New Yorker*.

Early in the 1970s Hans Koning moved to London in what he has called a "self-imposed exile," and turned from fiction to political writing. In the fall of 1980 he returned to the United States for good. This is the first novel of his "new life" as a novelist.